Chasing Redbird

Sharon Creech is an American who has lived in England for 19 years. She now lives in New Jersey, USA, where her husband is headmaster of a boarding school. In addition to *Chasing Redbird*, Sharon Creech has written four other novels for children, including *Walk Two Moons*.

Chasing Redbird was shortlisted for both the 1997 Whitbread Children's Book of the Year and the Children's Book Award 1997.

Praise for *Chasing Redbird*:

'It only takes Sharon Creech three and a half pages to set the mood and surroundings of *Chasing Redbird*. After that you will hardly want to let go . . . Sharon Creech won the hearts of younger teens with her previous book, *Walk Two Moons*, and this eagerly awaited novel is no disappointment.'
The Times

'Magnificent storytelling by an author with an understanding of a child's astonishing ability sometimes to think of very little, and sometimes to think deep, impenetrable thoughts.'
The Scotsman

'A bright, deep novel for teenagers.'
The Observer

' . . . the sort of influences we should be begging for – genuinely stirring adventures in settings far removed from bland surburbia.'
Times Educational Supplement

SHARON CREECH

Chasing Redbird

MACMILLAN CHILDREN'S BOOKS

First published 1997 by Macmillan Children's Books

This edition published 1997 by Macmillan Children's Books
a division of Macmillan Publishers Limited
25 Eccleston Place, London SW1W 9NF
Basingstoke and Oxford

Associated companies throughout the world

ISBN 0 330 34213 4

5 7 9 8 6 4

A CIP catalogue record for this book is available from
the British Library.

Phototypeset by Intype London Ltd
Printed by Mackays of Chatham plc, Chatham, Kent

Acknowledgement
'Boogie Woogie Bugle Boy', by Don Raye and Hughie Prince © 1940 MCA
Music Publishing, a division of MCA Inc. Renewed 1967.

For Lyle

With thanks to K.T.H.

OHIO

CHOCTON

FINISH

Surrender
Bridge

Doolittle Creek

Donut
Hole

Shady
Death
Ridge

Bear Alley Creek

Cab

Hogback Hill

Bear
Alley

Sleepy
Bear
Ridge

Spook Hollow
DO NOT CROSS
AT NIGHT!

BYBANKS ~
CHOCTON
TRAIL

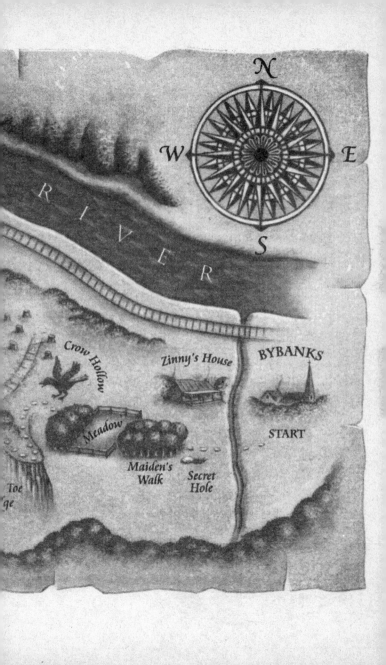

Contents

1

Tangled Spaghetti

Worms dangled in Aunt Jessie's kitchen: red worms swarming over a lump of brown mud in a bowl. The bowl and the worms and the lump of mud were in a cross-stitched picture hanging above the stove.

When I learned to read, I made out these words in blue letters beneath the bowl: *Life is a bowl of spaghetti* . . . Those worms weren't worms; they were spaghetti. I imagined myself rummaging among the twisted strands of pasta. That was my life?

There were more words: . . . *every now and then you get a meatball.* That mud was a meatball! I saw that meatball as a tremendous bonus you might unearth in all those convoluted spaghetti strands of your life. It was something to look forward to, a reward for all that slogging through your pasta.

In my thirteen years, I've had meatballs, and I've had lumps of mud, too.

My name is Zinny (for Zinnia) Taylor. I live with a slew of brothers and sisters and my parents on a farm in Bybanks, Kentucky. Our house fits snug up against Uncle Nate and Aunt Jessie's, the two houses yoked together like one. Sometimes it seems too crowded on our side, and you don't know who you are. You

1

feel like everybody's spaghetti is all tangled in one pot.

Last spring I discovered a trail at the back of our property – an old trail, overgrown with grass and weeds. I knew instantly that it was *mine and mine alone*. What I didn't know was how long it was or how hard it would be to uncover the whole thing, or that it would turn into such an obsession, that I'd be as driven as a chicken-eating dog in a henhouse.

This trail was just like the spaghetti of me and my family, of Uncle Nate and Aunt Jessie, and of Jake Boone. It took a heap of doing to untangle it.

2

The Quiet Zone

Strolling from our kitchen through the passage into Aunt Jessie and Uncle Nate's kitchen was like drifting back in time. On our side was a zoo of noises: the clomps and clumps of Ben, Will, and Sam zinging up and down the stairs; the blasting of Bonnie's stereo; the bleeping of Gretchen's computer; and the phone clanging off the wall for May.

But when you stepped through the passage, suddenly you'd be in the Quiet Zone of Aunt Jessie and Uncle Nate's house: silent as a tomb most of the time. There you'd see old-fashioned needlepoint pillows and wall hangings embroidered with poems and proverbs; you'd smell cinnamon and nutmeg; and you could trail your fingers over smooth counters and soft quilts.

I spent a lot of time in the Quiet Zone. My brothers and sisters didn't like it there, but I'd come to regard Uncle Nate and Aunt Jessie, his *Redbird*, as my second parents. They didn't have any children now, though once they'd had a daughter named Rose, who was born the same month and year that I was.

When Rose and I were four years old, I got whooping cough, and then Rose caught it from me.

Rose had it bad, bad, bad. When she died, Aunt Jessie did a strange thing. She whipped out the bottom drawer of her huge dresser, plonked the drawer on a table, and lined it with Rose's pink baby quilt. She placed Rose inside, and lit a dozen candles on the mantelpiece.

Aunt Jessie believed that a newborn baby's first bed should be a dresser drawer (pulled out from the dresser, though), and a person's last bed, before her coffin, should be a dresser drawer. If you put a dead person in a dresser drawer, she would be reborn as an innocent babe. Aunt Jessie had some peculiar beliefs.

I kept sneaking in to look at Rose, waiting for her to blink her sleepy eyes and sit up. People said, 'Don't touch her!' but I did, once. I tapped her hand, and it scared the beans out of me. It wasn't *her* hand. It was like a doll's hand, stiff, neither warm nor cold. I studied my own hand, wondering if it was going to turn into a doll's hand like Rose's.

For two days, people filed in and out of that room, weeping over Rose in the dresser drawer. In my four-year-old mind, I knew I was responsible for Rose being in that drawer, and I waited for someone to punish me. Instead, people kept asking me if I was feeling better, and telling me how lucky I was. I didn't feel very lucky. I felt like it was me in that drawer, or as if someone was going to lift Rose out and put me in instead.

You might think that because Rose had caught the whooping cough from me, and I was still living, that Aunt Jessie and Uncle Nate would hold it against me, but they didn't seem to. Instead, they took me on as their own special responsibility. I was a sickly, pathetic child, who caught every germ that floated through the house. Every time I got sick, Aunt Jessie would bundle me up and take me to her house and nurse me until I got better.

Sometimes she called me Rose instead of Zinny, which made me feel peculiar. I wondered if maybe I *was* Rose; maybe it was Zinny who had died, and I was Rose, and these were my real parents.

My mother was having babies right and left, and maybe she felt guilty that she had so many children while Aunt Jessie and Uncle Nate had none. Maybe she also felt, as I later came to feel, that we owed Aunt Jessie and Uncle Nate something. In any case, my parents let them fuss over me, and I liked being at their house, although I avoided that drawer. It was back in the dresser, but I'd imagine horrid things in it: dead bodies, especially.

When I wasn't sick, Aunt Jessie and Uncle Nate would take me on health walks around the farm. Uncle Nate might point out that because a red oak had open pores, its wood was used to make barrels that would hold dry things, but a white oak's pores oozed sticky gum that formed a tight seal, so with white oak you could make ships. He and Aunt Jessie were regular walking encyclopedias.

'Bingo!' Aunt Jessie would say, bending down to point out a buttercup or a fern. She'd pick up a plant fossil and tell me how it got there, millions of years ago. 'What a wonder!' The only things she didn't think were wonders were snakes. She'd flinch at the sight of a crooked twig, mistaken for a snake. 'That's one thing I can't abide,' she'd say. 'A snake is not a wonder to me. I don't know how God could have made such a creature.'

At the end of our health walks, we'd pass the family cemetery where Rose was buried, but they never went too close to her grave. It was a strange thing about Rose. It was as if they'd erased her. All her toys were gone, all her clothes, all her pictures. I was having trouble remembering her. It was as if everything to do with Rose was put away in a drawer in my mind, and I couldn't open that drawer.

Sometimes I'd go to the cemetery by myself and drape flowers on Rose's headstone. I'd talk to Rose, telling her what had been happening, and asking her how she was doing. This was a major accomplishment for me, because I hardly ever spoke to live people.

It wasn't that I was stupid (although a lot of teachers thought so when I first entered their classes), or that I didn't like people. It was just that there didn't seem to be a lot to say that someone wasn't already saying. I liked listening.

3

Sinking

Our Aunt Jessie was snatched away from us six months ago. In the middle of a cool spring night, she up and died. It was a terrible, terrible time.

Her death, so sudden and unexpected, left us all dazed and jittery, as we stumbled around trying to get our bearings. It was as if we'd all been slapped, hard, by a giant hand swooping down from the sky.

Uncle Nate took to wandering around the whole livelong day and sometimes the night, taking photographs and talking to himself and to invisible people. One of them was his *Redbird*, Aunt Jessie, and he spent most of his time trying to catch her. Sometimes he'd chase her through the field, only we couldn't see her, just him, loping along with a gnarled stick in his hand. He wasn't trying to hit her. He always carried that stick.

The stick was to beat the snakes with. I'd only ever seen one snake on our farm – a snake *I* had brought down from my trail – but still, Uncle Nate kept in practice. He whacked at anything that remotely resembled a snake. Once I caught him beating a belt, which was lying on the floor, nearly half to death. Another time I saw him beating the clothes line. I don't know what he thought a snake would be doing strung up in the air like that with shirts hanging off it.

And me, I figured Aunt Jessie's death was all my fault, because of things I'd done and said. There I was: *Zinnia Taylor: agent of doom*. I felt as if someone had tied me up and dropped me in the middle of a swamp, where I was in danger of sinking like a discarded meatball. I was like a walking mummy, all sealed up against the world, sinking, sinking, sinking.

It was about a month after her death that Jake Boone came back. We've always known Jake's family, just as we've always known everyone else around here. Four or five years ago, Jake's parents split up, and his mother took Jake and moved away, leaving Jake's father all by himself. Then, shortly after Aunt Jessie died, Jake came back and tried to get me out of that swamp. He sure had an odd way of going about it, though.

4

One-day Special

Jake Boone used to be a skinny little kid ('as skinny as six o'clock,' Aunt Jessie said), and all I remembered about him was that once he cried at church when my sister May pushed him into a hedge because he'd tried to give her a daffodil. When Jake moved away, I forgot all about him, and that is the up-and-down truth.

The next time I saw Jake was after Aunt Jessie died, when I went into Mrs Flint's store one Friday afternoon. Behind the counter was a tall, broad-shouldered boy, who looked about sixteen years old (which is how old he was.) He was wearing a white T-shirt with the sleeves rolled up, which is not the way boys wear their T-shirts in this town. His hair was short and dark, and he smiled a big smile at me.

'Howdy,' he said. 'Which one are you?'

I'm used to this question, but I didn't answer.

'I know you're a Taylor,' he said, 'because you look like a Taylor. But which one are you? Gretchen? May?'

'Zinny.' I was surprised at the sound of my own voice, which I hadn't used much lately.

'Naw! Can't be! You were just a scrawny little pipsqueak when I saw you last.'

'And when was that?' I asked.

'Heck – I haven't seen you since the hogs et Grandma.'

Hogs didn't really eat his grandma. That's just a Bybanks expression.

'Don't you know who I am?' he said.

'Maybe I do and maybe I don't.' (I didn't.)

'Jake – I'm Jake!'

I looked him over. 'Jake Boone?'

'Yep.' He put both hands against his chest, as if he were making sure he was still there. 'That's me, all right.'

He didn't look anything like that skinny little dirt dauber that May had stuck in the hedge.

'What are you staring at?' he asked. 'Don't you believe it's me?'

I didn't. I thought maybe he was an impostor. You never know. In a movie I once saw, a lady's husband came back from the war, and it took her two years to figure out that the man wasn't her real husband after all. 'You look different.'

'Well, so do you,' he said. 'How's your family? Sorry to hear about your aunt. How's Uncle Nate taking it?'

'Hard.'

'How's May and Bonnie and Will? And Gretchen? Ben? Sam?'

He sure had a good memory. 'Fine,' I said.

'And Sal Hiddle? You two still best friends?'

'She's gone,' I said. 'Ohio.' That was another big empty hole in my life. My best friend Sal had been forced to move to Ohio with her father. Sal insisted that she was coming back to Bybanks, but I wasn't convinced. That's what her mother had said once, and her mother sure hadn't returned.

'Who's living at their place? I saw a car there—'

'People named Butler. Renting,' I said.

'Your sister May – she still have that hot temper?'

'Hotter than a boiled owl,' I said.

Jake picked up the flour I'd put on the counter. 'This all you need?' He rang it up, put the flour in a bag, snatched a package of cookies from the shelf behind him, and dropped them in the bag too.

'You didn't charge me enough,' I said, 'and I didn't ask for cookies.'

'You're sharp as a fence post, Zinny Taylor.' He pushed the bag across the counter. 'Flour's on sale today. And when you buy flour, you get a free bag of cookies.'

'Mrs Flint never does that.'

'New policy,' Jake said. 'It's a one-day special.' Just before I left, he added, 'Maybe I'll come on up and see you sometime.'

'Somebody's always there,' I said, figuring he meant my whole family.

At dinner that night, my mother said, 'Where'd those cookies come from – the ones on the counter?'

I explained about the one-day special.

Dad said, 'Mrs Flint did that? A special?'

'No, Jake Boone.'

My sister May, who is sixteen and proud of it, said, 'Jake Boone? He's back? That skinny little doodlebug—'

11

Dad said, 'I heard he and his mother are both back.'

'For good?' Mom asked.

'Back home with Mr Boone?' Gretchen asked.

'That's what I hear,' Dad said.

In the middle of this, Uncle Nate sat quietly at one end of the table. He was waving at the gravy bowl, so I passed it along to him.

May pressed on. 'What's that doodlebug Jake like?'

'Different,' I said.

Gretchen, my oldest sister, said, 'Is he handsome?'

Everyone looked at me. I shrugged. 'Don't know.' (I did know. He was.)

May said, 'Well, is he gonna come up and visit us?'

I said, 'Maybe.'

'Honestly, Zinny,' May said, 'you ought to learn how to talk in complete sentences. When's he coming?'

'Don't know. Sometime.'

You might just as well roll over and die when May sets her sights on someone. She gets all the boys. *All* of them. You get mashed flatter than a fritter if you get in her way.

5

Resolutions

The centre of the town of Bybanks is about a mile away from our house. There are three small school buildings and a grocery store, gas station, church, and post office. That's it. There are a hundred and twenty-two people spread out in Bybanks, according to the sign at the town limits, and nearly everyone lives on a farm. Kids from nearby towns go to our schools; otherwise there'd only be about a dozen students, and most of them would be Taylors.

Stretching out behind our farm are hills – thirty, forty, maybe fifty miles of nothing but hills and trees and rivers. People around here say that you can slip up into the hills and wander for days, weeks, months, and not see another living soul. They say there are places back in the hills that have never been trodden by human feet.

Our farm has always belonged to Uncle Nate, who is Dad's much-older brother – or maybe it belonged to Dad. It was a steady argument as to whose farm it was. Uncle Nate would say it was Dad's farm, and Dad insisted it was Nate's until the day Nate kicked the bucket.

Uncle Nate was a restless man, as frisky as a flea on an old barn dog, and sometimes he used to drive

Aunt Jessie crazy, getting in her way. During these times, she would suggest he take one of his mountain treks or else work the farm more. He'd usually choose the mountain trek, and he'd say, 'Sure you won't come with me?' Sometimes she'd relent and join him, but increasingly she'd heave a big sigh and tell him to go on alone. She always said she had a weak heart, and she had diabetes – which she called her *sugar*. 'My sugar's acting up,' she'd say.

Uncle Nate would say, 'Guess I'll go on alone and meet my sweetheart.' I never paid any attention to that; I figured he was joking.

When Uncle Nate went off into the hills, he'd sometimes be gone the whole day, and now and then he'd even take a sleeping bag and camp overnight. He rarely chose to work the farm, because he had his resolutions about farming.

He once tried to raise chickens, but then decided he couldn't bear to see them killed, so he made a resolution not to raise chickens anymore. Next, he grew tobacco. Our land is perfect for tobacco, as it is moist, dark earth that gets a fair amount of sun and rain. Although Uncle Nate liked his smoke every now and then, he got worried when the Surgeon General said that tobacco was dangerous to everybody's health, and so he made a resolution that he would not raise tobacco.

We had a whole big herd of dairy cows for a while, but they got a disease and we lost twenty-seven in two days. Uncle Nate said he couldn't bear to see such sweet creatures die, and so he made a resolution not to keep cows, except for two which gave us our milk.

Pigs would be like chickens and have to be slaughtered, so he made a resolution about pigs. Corn and tomatoes were next. Uncle Nate practically gave them away at the market, being unable to charge hardly anything for them, as this was against his resolution not to cheat people. Aunt Jessie finally told him to quit planting them, as they were going to waste and we were losing our shirts. So now corn and tomatoes were OK, but not in too much abundance, only what we could eat ourselves and give to the neighbours. Since we didn't make much money off of Uncle Nate's efforts on the farm, it was a good thing my dad worked full time as manager of the county airport.

Aunt Jessie was a redhead, which is how she got her nickname Redbird from Uncle Nate, and because of her red hair she stood out from the rest of us. Uncle Nate and Dad were sort of average-looking, but all of us kids looked like my mother: dark hair, dark eyes, little noses and ears, long skinny legs. Mom once said she felt like a photocopy machine. She said this to Mrs Flint, one day in the grocery store, and Mrs Flint must have thought Mom was complaining about the number of children she had, because Mrs Flint said, 'Ain't you ever been told about birth control? A person doesn't have to have a million kids, you know. You can go to the doctor and get a pill.'

Aunt Jessie was with us at the time, and she said,

'Doctor, schmoctor. God gave her these children, and if God wants to give her a pill, then let Him do it.'

It was a sensitive issue, and I wouldn't have touched it with a ten-foot pole, so as usual I kept my mouth shut.

6

Tadpoles and Pumpkins

The day I'd seen Jake Boone at the store, May stood up after dinner and said, 'I'm tired of people asking me which Taylor I am. I'm tired of you all saying "Bonnie – Gretchen – Zinny – May" before figuring out which one you're talking to.'

May was launching into one of her rages, but I knew exactly what she meant. My parents were always saying, 'Bon-Gret-May-Zinny?' or 'Will-Ben-Sam?'

May plunged on. 'I'm going to make it easy for you to remember exactly which one I am.' She waggled a striped ribbon in her hair. 'It's multi-coloured,' she said. '*M* is for *m*ulti-coloured and for *M*ay.' I thought she was a bit old for hair ribbons, but apparently she'd seen a magazine article that said that ribbons were back in style. May was big on style.

Gretchen, who is seventeen, then announced she would wear only green ('*G* is for green and Gretchen,' she said). This wouldn't be a big hardship for her, because green had always been her favourite colour.

Eleven-year-old Bonnie decided to wear only *blue*. This did not leave me with a good option, as I could not think of any colours beginning with Z. Bonnie suggested I paint a zinnia (it's a flower) on all my clothes.

That night I did exactly that. When I went downstairs, with a newly painted red zinnia on my shirt, my mother looked at that *red* flower, obviously puzzled. In her tired mind, she was probably trying to remember if she had named one of her children something beginning with *R*. *Rebecca*? *Ruby*? Or did the *flower* mean my name began with *F*? Had she named me *Fanny*? *Frances*?

'It's a zinnia, Mom. I'm Zinny.'

'I know it,' she said. 'I can tell you all apart. It's just that my head is full of other things. If I were blindfolded and you walked in the room, I'd know it was you.'

'How?'

'Because I know who Zinny is. I know what she sounds like, smells like. I know what she . . . radiates. I know who she *is*.'

I wanted to ask *And who is that*?, but I didn't.

'Anyway, Zinny,' she said, 'that's not a zinnia you've painted. That's a rose, isn't it?'

What do you know about that? I'd gone and painted a rose on my shirt. It was spooky.

My younger brothers took a different approach. Will (he's ten) decided to eat only *w*hite foods (rice, potatoes, bread, the whites of eggs, etc.); *B*en (he's nine) would eat *b*eans with every meal, even breakfast; and *S*am (at seven, the youngest) chose *s*oup. It wouldn't necessarily make it easier to tell them apart unless you were at the dinner table with them, but you could usually count on the fact that some of their food would be on their clothes, and so that might give you a hint.

Mom and Dad made an effort to use these hints and call us by our right names, but Uncle Nate didn't even try. He had always called all the boys *tadpole* (sometimes referring to 'the littlest tadpole' or 'the biggest tadpole') and all of us girls *pumpkin*. I can assure you that Gretchen was not thrilled to be known as 'the biggest pumpkin'.

Except for my brother Ben, my sisters and brothers liked to be inside with the computer and television and stereo and phone. Ben and I would rather be outdoors, especially since I got healthier. I hadn't had a cold or anything like that in years. The worst punishment was to have to clean the house or stay in my room. 'There isn't enough *air* in there,' Aunt Jessie used to say, and I agreed. She and I did a lot of inside things outside: peel potatoes, sort laundry, fold clothes. We even ironed outside, as long as it wasn't raining, and she had a twenty-foot-long extension cord that ran from her kitchen to the outside, just for this purpose.

I shared a room with my three sisters, and at night, when May and Gretchen thought Bonnie and I were both asleep, they would whisper. Once I heard them playing the *-est* game. It went like this:

May whispered, 'So what am I? You're the oldest and smartest, Gretchen. Everyone knows that.'

'You're the prettiest, May.'

'Do you really think so?'

'Of course. Everyone does.'

19

'And Bonnie – she's the nicest,' May said.

'Will's the strongest, and Ben's the gentlest, don't you think?' Gretchen asked.

'Yes, and Sam, he's the cutest.'

'What about Zinny?' Gretchen asked. 'We forgot Zinny.'

'She's the . . . the . . . *strangest* and *stingiest* dirt-daubing doodlebug!'

They laughed and laughed.

7

The Trail

The day after I saw Jake at Mrs Flint's store was Saturday. Dad and Uncle Nate were up in the field setting out tomato plants. They'd left a tray of plants down by the 'squirt gardens' behind the house. These were the mini-gardens that each of us kids kept, and the week before, I had planted zinnias around the border of mine. I didn't like to see that lonely brown earth, so plain and bare like the top of Aunt Jessie's grave.

There were three rules for our squirt gardens: We could plant whatever we wanted; we had to take care of our own gardens (weeding and watering and de-bugging); and we could do whatever we wanted with what we grew, which was basically eat it or sell it. The first year I planted mine, I was so selfish with what I grew that I wouldn't even let *myself* eat any of it, and I sure as heck wasn't going to give it to anyone else. Then I cried when it all went rotten.

That Saturday, I planted and watered six tomato plants in my squirt garden, and then told each plant it would be OK. Aunt Jessie had firmly believed that if you treated each plant as an individual, it would be a happier plant and give you more tomatoes.

When I was finished, I snuck off, raced up the hill

behind the barn and down the other side, and ran along the creek until I came to the start of my trail. I felt like I owned the trail because I had discovered it. Actually I had *re*discovered it, a few weeks before Aunt Jessie died. The trail had been there for at least two hundred years.

I had found it by accident when I was poking along the creek bank, following a sleepy frog. It wasn't a very clever frog, for he leaped away from the water into the grass and soon was tangled up in it. That's when I stepped on something hard, which shifted beneath me, slurping in the mud. It was a large, flat piece of slate, covered with dead leaves and grass.

When I moved back, there was another slurp as I stepped on a slab laid end to end with the first one. For the next few hours, I cleared away grass and debris, uncovering a row of similar stones, leading in a line from the river on up the hill. *Zinnia Taylor: explorer!*

For a few days, I kept my discovery a secret, wanting to have something of my own, but Ben and Sam followed me one day, and when they saw my newly uncovered trail – which, by this time, was half a mile long – they raced back to get Will and Bonnie. Soon the whole family was up there, stepping along the stones. Everybody was flapping around, saying, 'What is it?' and 'Where'd it come from?' and 'Who did it?' and 'Where does it go?'

Only Uncle Nate and Aunt Jessie were quiet. Uncle Nate was kicking the stones and looking all around, as if he'd just landed on this planet. At last he said,

'I never heard such a noisy bunch of tadpoles and pumpkins in all my born days.'

'Do you know what it is?' Dad asked.

'It's the dag-blasted trail,' Uncle Nate said.

'*What* dag-blasted trail?'

'*The* dag-blasted trail. Goes nowhere.'

'It must go *somewhere*,' Will said.

'Goes nowhere,' Aunt Jessie said, echoing Uncle Nate.

'I'm going to walk the whole thing,' Gretchen said.

'Me too!' Will agreed.

I don't know what came over me. 'You can't go,' I said. 'It's covered. Only this part is cleared because *I* cleared it. It's mine.'

'Don't be a toad,' Will said. 'It isn't yours.'

I felt as if he were robbing me of my most prized possession. There was something about the trail – I couldn't have said what – that was suddenly so important to me that I became determined to defend it. 'I discovered it. I cleared it.'

'You didn't discover it. It was already here. You just found it again. Big deal. I might have found it, if I'd been out here,' Will said.

'I did all the work.'

Will glared at me. 'You didn't uncover the whole thing yet. I can uncover some.'

'Me too,' Bonnie said.

I'd had plans for my trail, and now they were all taking it over.

Uncle Nate repeated, 'Goes nowhere.' Aunt Jessie seemed uneasy – because she didn't want us all wandering off into the hills, I figured, but I was wrong. Uncle Nate and Aunt Jessie knew what was on that trail, and they didn't want anyone else to find it.

Not long after this, I discovered the maps. Our class took a field trip to a local historical museum, and I hate to say it, but it was the most boring place on this earth. It was dark and musty inside, and you walked around and looked in glass cases which held tiny bits of broken pottery and yellowed books and portraits of old people. Just as I thought I was going to perish from being held captive in that dark room, I wandered over to one exhibit and stared inside at a map. I saw a dotted line, and my eyes followed it across the map, and across these words: *Bybanks–Chocton Trail.*

The Bybanks–Chocton Trail! I studied the map. The portion in the case showed the start of it, at Bybanks, just down the road from our farm, but it didn't show our farm or the rest of the trail. When I asked the guide if there were any more of these maps, she led me downstairs to a cobwebby, dark room, with only a single light bulb hanging from the ceiling. Here were books of maps, loose maps, big maps, little maps – all yellow, all dusty. It didn't take us long to find other maps of the Bybanks–Chocton Trail, and at last we had three separate ones that showed it from start to finish: a twenty-mile trail. We photocopied the maps, and I brought them home and hid them in the back of my closet, underneath my bottle-cap collection. No one ever looked there.

For the next week, I studied these maps every day,

memorizing every inch of them. I found the place where our farm was now, the creek, and the stretch of trail I'd already uncovered. They were primitive maps, rough sketches of the trail's course with hand-written legends and names of places that sounded both fabulous and strange. I envisioned myself gliding through Maiden's Walk and Crow Hollow. I'd forge my way along Baby Toe Ridge and recline on Sleepy Bear Ridge. I wasn't so sure about Spook Hollow and Shady Death Ridge, however.

Twice, I returned to the museum, where I learned that the route had originally been an Indian trail, later used by trappers, and later still by loggers. A now busted railroad, set up by a logging company to haul timber down from the hills, ran across the trail near the midpoint.

It was a narrow trail, wide enough for men on horseback, but too narrow for wagons. The lower portions of my trail were laid with stone slabs. The museum guide said this was to make travel easier during the spring, when the ground was muddy and swampy. She also said that settlers had blazed a wider wagon route down near the river, following its meandering course, and that that had evolved into the main road between Bybanks and Chocton.

In the museum, I also found faded photos of people riding on my trail, and each time I set out to clear a new section of the trail, I wondered about these people. Who were they? What were they thinking? Why were they going to Bybanks or to Chocton?

*

On that day that I planted tomatoes in my squirt garden, I made my way along the mile of the trail that I'd already cleared. Down below me was the farm, our house, the long gravel drive leading to the main road, and beyond were pale rolling hills swooping to the Ohio River, soupy brown from the recent April rains which had swept the bare soil into it.

When I reached the place where I'd last stopped clearing, I found my trowel wedged beneath a bush. The trowel and a hoe were the only tools I had, beside my own two hands, but that's all I needed. I'd pull and scrape, clearing one stone at a time. This was easiest right after a rain, when the earth was loose around the roots of the weeds, or when, for some mysterious reason, the weeds had skipped over a stone and left it nearly bare. But usually it was not so easy, and I'd have to wrench and tug to pull the weeds loose.

Sometimes I'd lie back in the grass and watch the clouds and listen to the deep, dark woods which stretched behind me. The trail was curving in the direction of those woods, and part of me was eager to enter them to see where the trail would lead, and part of me was pigeon-hearted, uneasy about what might await me there.

Clearing the trail was slow work that day. On my way home, when I rounded the bend where I could see the farm below, I noticed Mr Boone's truck parked beside the barn. During the time his wife and Jake had been away, lonely Mr Boone had often come to our house. But we'd not seen him since his wife and Jake had come back, and I was surprised that his truck was there.

I made my way down the hill, stopping to check the newly planted tomatoes in the squirt garden, and headed for the house. It may have been Mr Boone's truck there, but it wasn't Mr Boone who was visiting.

8
Bottle Caps

'Guess who's on the porch,' Bonnie said.

'Mr Boone,' I said.

'Wrong.'

'Mrs Boone, then.'

'Wrong.'

'So who is it?'

'Guess.'

You can never get a straight answer out of Bonnie. The whole family was on the porch, even Uncle Nate, and with them was Jake Boone. Everybody was yapping at him a mile a minute, asking him so many questions you'd have thought he was Elvis Presley himself dropping in for a visit. May was sitting next to him on the porch swing, gazing at him dreamily and twirling her hair ribbon. They didn't see me right away.

'So you're working at Flint's store?' Dad was asking.

'Yep, I am,' Jake said.

'How much they paying you?' Uncle Nate demanded. Since Aunt Jessie had died, he'd sometimes act irritable and grumpy like this, as if people were annoying him by simply being alive.

Jake told him his hourly wage.

'Highway robbery!' Uncle Nate said.

'It's the minimum wage,' Jake said.

'Highway robbery. I never made that much in a whole dag-blasted week. Dag-blasted inflation. We oughta run them poll-u-ticians out of the country. We oughta—'

'Hey, Zinny!' Jake said. As he stood up, the swing bumped against the back of his legs. May gave me a sour look.

'You're welcome to stay on for dinner,' Mom said.

Jake thanked her, but he had to get to work.

'This time of day?' Uncle Nate said. 'Stores oughta be closing at this time of day. Shouldn't be open on a Saturday night. People oughta be at home doing their chores, being with their family. You tell that to Mrs Flint, you hear?'

Jake stepped off the porch and poked me in the side. 'I can't get over you, Zinny. You sure have changed.'

May followed him as if she were attached to him with a string. 'Do you think *I've* changed, Jake?' she asked.

'Not a bit,' he said, and May blushed. 'Want to see my truck, Zinny?'

'Your dad's truck?' I said. 'Seen it before.'

'I want to show you something.'

'I'll come too,' May said.

On the floor of the truck was a small cardboard box, which Jake handed to me.

May reached for the box. 'Here, I'll open it.'

Jake said, 'It's for Zinny.'

'For *Zinny*?' May shrank back as if he had slapped

her, and when I opened the box, she said, 'Bottle caps?'

'You still collect those?' Jake asked me.

'Sure.' I didn't know what else to say. I didn't know what to think about Jake and his present.

'Bottle caps?' May said, stuck on those words.

As Jake drove off, May waved delicately at the back end of the truck. 'Honestly, Zinny, you're too old to be collecting bottle caps. It's so embarrassing. A person could die of embarrassment with you around.'

Into my mind flew Tommy Salami. His real name was Tom Salome, but even he called himself Tommy Salami. Three years ago he was in May's class at school, but whenever he saw me, he'd give me a present. They were bitty things: a plastic ring from a cereal box; an old bottle from his barn; and a rusty key he'd found along the road. To me, they were treasures, and I got the dizzies just thinking about him.

He would say the most unusual things. He asked me if I'd ever seen trees walk, and if I'd ever wanted to be an aquarium.

'An *aquarium*?' I said. 'You mean something in it – a fish?'

'No, I mean the *whole* aquarium. Everything: the water, the plants, the fish, the snails – an aquarium.'

I worshipped Tommy Salami. I thought of him day and night, I dreamed about him, and I wrote his name in all my school books. As far as I was concerned, Tommy Salami had hung the moon and stars; that's how great I thought he was.

Then one day, I saw him walking up our drive. I could barely breathe: Tommy Salami was coming to my house. Tommy Salami was coming to see *me*. Quick as a dog can lick a dish, I whipped a brush through my hair, changed my shirt and ran downstairs. I pushed through the screen door, and there on the porch swing was Tommy Salami. Beside him was May.

I crept back inside, stumbled through the house and out the other side. I made my way down the drive and waited. One hour. Two. At last, I saw Tommy Salami leaving, and I stepped out.

'Zinny?' he said. 'Where did *you* come from?'

I didn't answer. There weren't any words.

'I owe you some thanks,' he said. 'You must've put in a good word about me with May. She's going to the dance with me. How 'bout that?' He had a grin so wide you'd have thought he had a couple extra sets of teeth. 'You're a real peach, Zinny.'

All I could think was that I was *Zinnia Taylor: idiot.* I was mortally embarrassed and certain-sure I'd die in my sleep of complete and total humiliation. I didn't amount to a bucket of spit.

There were more boys like Tommy Salami. There was Jerry Abbott and Mickey Torke, Slim Giblin and Roger Pole. They all plied me with sugar-mouthed flattery and gifts, and they all eventually ended up with May. I might as well have been a pig in a dog race.

I don't know why these boys didn't try to go through Gretchen or Bonnie to win May, or why they didn't just pursue her directly. I guess Gretchen

31

gave off this air that she wouldn't put up with any nonsense, and Bonnie was probably too young. And maybe these boys were afraid of May, afraid she'd turn them down. Nobody was afraid of me. I must have seemed as quiet and as harmless as a mothball.

But after Tommy Salami, I was not as trusting, and by the time poor old Roger Pole came along, I was downright nasty. When he offered me a bag of popcorn, I threw a double duck fit and said, 'Take your stupid popcorn and choke on it.'

After Jake gave me the bottle caps, I just felt sad. I sorted through them that evening. There were nearly a hundred. He'd found some rare soda tops, no longer made, and many I'd never seen before. They were all clean, and he must have known how to pop the insides, because none of them were bent. I added them to the others already in my closet.

I had lots of collections: lucky stones (small and smooth and white); zinnia seeds; key chains; buttons; coloured pencils; keys; shoelaces (all tied together in one long piece); bottles; bookmarks; postcards; and the bottle caps.

May said it was a sign of my stinginess, that I hoarded things like this. For me, it didn't feel like stinginess. It felt as if I were protecting these things. I wouldn't let anything happen to them. I wouldn't let anyone take them away.

These collections were sheltered in individual boxes crammed into the closet I shared with Bonnie. May called our closet 'the pig closet' because it was a mad jumble of things, while the closet May and

Gretchen shared at the other end of the room was so neat and tidy it was hard to believe people really used it.

That night after I had put away my new bottle caps, and the four of us girls were all in bed, with Bonnie fast asleep and me pretending to be, I listened to May and Gretchen whispering.

'Do you think Jake is handsome?' May asked.

'His hair is nice,' Gretchen said.

'And he has nice muscles.'

'Mm.'

They were quiet for a few minutes and I thought maybe they had gone to sleep, but then May said, 'I wish Zinny didn't collect things.'

'How come?'

'It's so . . . so immature, don't you think?'

'I collect green things,' Gretchen admitted.

'That's different. That's not immature. But bottle caps – now *that's* immature!'

They laughed.

Too bad, I thought. It made me even more determined to keep on collecting them. But then, in the quiet, in the dark, I wondered if they were right. Was I immature? Questions like this can keep you awake a long time.

9

Back in the Drawer

This is why I thought Aunt Jessie's death was my fault:

The day before Aunt Jessie died, I was up working on the trail. I was thinking about her because the anniversary of Rose's death was approaching, and Aunt Jessie always got very quiet around this time, very still, as if her whole body were holding itself in, as if she were suspending herself in time in order to get through this anniversary without disintegrating into a million pieces.

A cold wind reared up on the trail, sweeping heavy clouds overhead and dumping hail on me. I huddled beneath a pine tree near the path, watching the hail become bigger and bigger, sailing down from the clouds and whacking into the ground, bouncing in all directions. A thick layer of pine needles carpeted the ground around me, and I trailed my trowel through them.

When the trowel hit something hard, I scraped the pine needles away, uncovering a flat piece of slate, similar to that used along the trail. It was odd for the slate to be there, some twenty feet away from the trail. I cleared a wider space, but there was only this single slab set in the dirt.

Clumps of mud and a worm clung to the bottom of the slab. As I dug in the space beneath where the stone had been, the trowel snagged something. I unearthed a small leather pouch with a drawstring around its neck. Inside was a gold coin.

What a discovery! Suddenly I was *Zinnia Taylor: famous archaeologist*, single-handedly responsible for the discovery of the century. On closer examination, it didn't seem to be a coin at all, but some sort of medallion. On one side was the outline of a woman's head, and on the other side was a man's head and these engraved initials: *TNWM*.

I had the strangest sense that I'd held this medallion before, and it was a creepy feeling. Seeing it in my palm like that reminded me of something, something – but what? Had I been here long ago, maybe in another life? Had I held this coin? Had I seen someone bury it? I didn't like the feeling, and so I slid the medallion back into the pouch and stuffed it in my jacket, and when the hail stopped, I returned to clearing the trail.

But I couldn't keep my mind on my work. I kept trying to guess what the initials *TNWM* stood for. Were they one person's initials, like maybe Thomas Newton William Morris? Or were they two people's initials, like maybe Tom Newton, Willa Morris? Did the initials stand for something else? *Time Never Will Move?*

When a second bank of dark clouds raised their heads in the distance, I raced for home. Along the way, a harmless little grass snake slithered across the trail and, impulsively, I snatched it up. *Zinnia*

Taylor: noted biologist captures rare species. In the barn I found an old coffee can wedged behind oil cans, dumped the sack of screws which it had contained, dropped the snake inside, and punched holes in the lid.

Aunt Jessie appeared at the barn door. 'I wondered where you'd got to,' she said. She was standing stiffly, her arms pressed against her sides.

'Look . . .' I brought out the leather pouch and handed it to her. 'It was under a rock along the trail.'

She opened the pouch and emptied the medallion into her palm.

'And look what else I found . . .'

Now why did I do this? I knew she was afraid of snakes. I knew it, but still I held it up to show her. Maybe I was proud of it. It was so small, so innocent looking, not like a *real* snake. But maybe, maybe, I wanted to tease her, to scare her a little bit, to make her not so stiff that day, to make her like the *other* Aunt Jessie. She glanced from the pouch in her hand to the snake in mine, took a step back, and let out a thin wail. She dropped the pouch and staggered back toward the doorway, as Uncle Nate entered.

That night, Aunt Jessie whipped out her bottom dresser drawer and plonked it in the middle of the room. She lined it with her marriage quilt and tried to curl up inside. She was a bit big for the drawer. Uncle Nate sat on the edge of the bed pleading with his Redbird to get out of that drawer, but it was as if she couldn't hear him, as if she'd already started on her journey.

I knew what that drawer meant, and I was scared to heaven and back. 'Please,' I begged her. 'Please . . .'

But she kept mumbling about *the hand of God* and calling me *Rose-baby, Rose-baby*, and my mother snatched me away and took me back to our side of the house.

In the middle of the night, according to my father, Aunt Jessie sat straight up and shouted, 'I hope it's a miracle I'm about to see!' and then she lay back and closed her eyes, and she was dead.

10

The Mission

Everybody was torn up about Aunt Jessie, but I think Uncle Nate and I took it the hardest. They let me see her the next morning. They'd taken her out of the drawer and put her on the bed. Uncle Nate was kneeling beside her, saying 'Redbird, Redbird,' over and over. I wanted to jump on the bed and pull her up, but she was lying still, just like Rose, and her hand looked just like Rose's, and it made me crazy. I had to get out of there. I had to get outside where there was air.

Later that day, I was alone in my room *(Zinnia Taylor: agent of doom)*, when Uncle Nate came in, carrying a stick.

'Where is it?' he demanded.

'Where's what?'

'That creature . . .' He thrashed his stick around the room, poking under the bed and dresser.

'In the closet,' I said.

'Get it.'

I pulled out the coffee can.

'Open it,' he said. 'Now pick it up by its tail. Now snap it like this . . .' He whipped his wrist in the air.

I did as he directed, holding the snake by the tail and whipping it in the air. There was one sharp snap, and then the snake hung lifeless. I dropped it and it lay still on the floor. 'What'd I do?'

'Killed it,' he said. Then he stood over it and thrashed the already dead snake with his stick, over and over and over. He was like a wild man, and I'd never in my life seen him like that. Usually he was the quietest, gentlest man you ever did see.

No one knew about the snake except me and Uncle Nate. I couldn't tell anyone. I didn't want anyone to know I'd killed Aunt Jessie. The doctor blamed her diabetes; he said her sugar was way out of sight. But I didn't believe it. How could anything so good as sugar kill a person?

For weeks, I hardly said a word to anyone. People buzzed around me like flies on a honey jar, knowing how close I'd been to Aunt Jessie, but their attention only made me feel worse. It kept reminding me of what I'd done and that I was *Zinnia Taylor: killer*. I had terrible, terrible nightmares in which people were chasing me through tall, stiff trees, and the farther I ran, the narrower were the spaces between the trees, so that I'd be squeezing myself through. I was afraid I'd get stuck and not be able to move and it would be then that the snakes would come and get me.

At home, I'd skulk around, trying not to be noticed, and yet hoping, wishing, praying to be noticed.

And Uncle Nate? In some ways he seemed the same: he'd putter around the house and yard, he'd sit on the porch, he'd talk in his same, quiet voice to us kids. And sometimes, even, he'd talk to me, just as he used to. 'Look here, pumpkin – look at this here rock I found,' he'd say.

But there were other times when he'd look at me and not seem to know who I was, and there were times he called me Rose, and as soon as he said that name, he'd stop and turn around and stare, as if someone else – Rose? Aunt Jessie? – were standing right beside me. And there were his bouts of grumpiness, when he seemed impatient with the world, and there were his chases, too, when off he'd go, running after his Redbird.

And my parents? They were so busy, as they always were, that it would be easy to think they weren't grieving for Aunt Jessie. My mother had always been distracted – simultaneously tying Sam's shoe and scooping up someone's muddy clothes and making out a grocery list and yelling at Will to get off the roof. But now she was bewildered, as if someone had spun her around and around, and then set her free to weave and wobble through our house.

She put the milk in the oven, and the sugar in the refrigerator. She lost her car keys every single day that first week. At least once a day, while Uncle Nate was out, she slipped into his house to tidy it up, and she'd come back with her eyes all red and puffy, and you'd know she'd been crying over Aunt Jessie. Sometimes she'd go out to Aunt Jessie's bare flower border, and just stand there, staring at the dirt.

For a while my father seemed as helpless as a turtle on its back. He took to digging in the garden a lot. This is not something he used to do very often, but in the first few weeks after Aunt Jessie died, you'd see him out there with his shovel and hoe, digging and scraping at the bare earth. At the dinner table, he'd turn to where Aunt Jessie used to sit and automatically say, 'Jess—' and then he'd catch himself and turn beet-red and try to cover it up by saying, 'Mess – what a mess that airport was today!' or 'Jest gonna get some more potatoes!' and we'd all look down at our plates and pretend we hadn't heard him.

My brothers and sisters? Well, Gretchen and May did a fair amount of whispering in the first few days after Aunt Jessie died, but as to what they said, I don't know. Will lay around the house like a rug, and absolutely never mentioned Aunt Jessie's name. I heard him tell Ben, 'I hate this bit about dying! I hate it!' and that's the only way I ever heard him refer to Aunt Jessie's death, as *this bit*.

Sam, the youngest, became obsessed with everything to do with funerals. He wanted to know where the coffin came from, and what it was made of, and if it was waterproof, and why did people send flowers, and did many people get buried alive, and why was the coffin put under the ground – why couldn't it be kept in the barn – on and on and on and on, until people started avoiding him because they couldn't bear to think about these things one more minute.

In a way, Ben seemed to be the calmest, and at first I thought he didn't mind too much. Later I found out that he had his own way of coping.

And by the time Jake Boone came to town, we were just beginning to emerge from our dazed states, like sleepy bears after a long, hard winter.

*

A few days after Aunt Jessie's funeral, I was up on the trail. To avoid thinking about Aunt Jessie, I kept trying to imagine the people who had ridden this trail all those many years ago. That's when an idea burst into my brain like fireworks exploding: I was going to uncover the whole trail and travel it on horseback.

There were a few problems with this, which I didn't consider at the time: to uncover twenty miles of trail was a hard job, and, secondly, I didn't have a horse to ride this trail even if I did clear it. At least I knew how to ride a horse. That I had learned at Sal Hiddle's farm, where she and I had spent whole days weaving through their woods on her horse, Willow. Unfortunately, Willow had been sold when the Hiddles moved to Ohio.

The more I thought about my plan, though, the bigger it got. This plan zipped through my brain like a dog tearing up the pea patch. Not only would I clear the trail, but I would plant zinnias all along the way, and it would become the Zinnia Bybanks–Chocton Trail, and everyone who saw the zinnias would think of me, Zinny, and be flabbergasted at what I had done. It would still be my trail, though, and people would have to ask permission to use it.

At the time, I thought this idea dropped down out of the blue, and I didn't know it would become so important. It didn't occur to me that I might be escaping something or even chasing something. It didn't occur to me that it would seem selfish. As for the zinnias and naming the trail after myself – well, I suppose I wanted to be known as something other than the *strangest and stingiest dirt-daubing doodlebug*, as something more than a little *mashed-up fritter at the bottom of the pot*. I suppose I wanted people to know exactly which Taylor I was, and for me to be something other than *Zinnia Taylor: killer.*

But I didn't know all this then. I only knew I had to undertake this mission. I *had* to. And I had to hurry, to complete it before the end of the summer, for in my morbid mind, I believed that if I didn't complete it by then, something horrible would happen. Whatever this horrible thing was would be a punishment for killing Aunt Jessie. I had decided that God had given me a chance – one chance – to redeem myself.

When an idea like that takes root in my brain, it grows like weeds on the riverbank.

And I needn't have worried about my brothers or sisters taking over my trail. They lost interest after a few days of clearing the debris, and it was mine once again.

11

Presents

On Sunday, the day after Jake had given me the bottle caps, I was outside at the squirt gardens when Jake returned. He said he'd just stopped by for a minute. In his hand was a small box, punctured with holes. 'Here,' he said, whisking it under my nose.

The contents of my stomach were tumbling around like socks in the clothes dryer. A present, from *Jake*. But then, in a flash, I thought, *Here we go again: another Tommy Salami bribing me with gifts so he can win May. I will not be swayed*.

'Open it,' he urged. 'It's for you. It's a thermometer.'

I lifted the lid and quickly replaced it. 'Very funny,' I said, handing it back. 'Looks more like a cricket to me.' Why did he have to look so eager? Why was he going to so much trouble when May was already falling all over herself trying to attract his attention?

'Which one of those windows is your room?' he asked.

Reluctantly, I played along, pretending I didn't know what he was really after. 'That one, up there. I share it with Bonnie and Gretchen and . . . May.'

'Where's your bed?'

'There – by that window. May's is by the other window.'

He didn't even flinch when I mentioned her name. *Stop it*! I wanted to yell at him. *Quit pretending*!

'Perfect,' he said, leading me to the oak tree which grows beside the house, its branches tapping against our bedroom window. 'See this tree?' He opened the box, tilting it against the trunk. The cricket hopped out and clung to the bark. Jake seemed mighty pleased with himself. He said, 'Do you have a clock near your bed? With a second hand?'

'Yes.'

'Now tonight, if you listen for this cricket and count the number of chirps in a minute, divide by four, and add thirty-seven, that'll be the temperature. Don't that beat all?!'

May surfaced as Jake's truck disappeared down the drive. 'Was that Jake? Where'd he go?'

'Don't know.'

'What'd he want? What'd he say?'

'Just fuss and feathers. Nothing special.'

'Did he ask for me?' May said.

Gretchen came outside. 'Was that Jake? What did he want?' May took her by the arm and led her toward the house, whispering. I didn't hear what May said, but Gretchen said, 'He's probably just shy. He probably wanted to ask for you, but he probably got embarrassed, that's all. He'll probably be back.'

A few minutes later, Bonnie emerged. 'May's mad at you,' she said. 'Guess why.' When I didn't answer, she said, 'May says you should have told her Jake was here. She says you don't have the sense of a flea.'

Uncle Nate ran by waving his stick. 'Hold on!' he yelled. 'Wait on up!'

'What are you chasing?' Bonnie called.

'My Redbird – look at her go!'

'Does he really see her?' Bonnie asked.

'Maybe . . .'

'Do you ever see her?'

'In my mind . . .' I admitted.

'But around here, do you see Aunt Jessie like Uncle Nate sees her?'

I wanted to be able to say yes. If he could see her, why couldn't I? 'Nope, I don't. Do you?'

'Of course not, but Ben does,' she said. 'Ben said he's seen Aunt Jessie twice since she was buried. Does he really? Or is he imagining it?'

Later, I found Ben sitting at the foot of his squirt garden, tilting his head to left and right. 'Are they straight?' he asked. 'Doesn't that third plant look a little crooked?'

'They're fine, Ben. Don't have to be exactly straight.'

'Yes they do.' Ben had decided to grow only beans in his garden, and he was very particular about his row. He liked it to be straight, and he would not allow any weeds whatsoever to grow in it. He checked it two or three times a day, and if he found a little weed trying to sprout up, he'd yell at it, 'Where'd you come from? Get on out of there!'

Once, when Ben was much younger, he told Aunt Jessie that he wanted 'the other kind of beans' too.

'What kind is that?' Aunt Jessie said.

'Human beans.'

Aunt Jessie explained that it was human beings, not human beans. Ben listened carefully and said, 'But maybe it really is human beans. Maybe if you took a little human egg and put it in the ground and watered it, it might grow.'

'Into what?' Aunt Jessie asked.

'A human bean, of course.'

Ben asked if I were going up to my trail.

'Yes,' I said, 'but don't tell anyone.'

'It must be getting long, Zinny,' he said. 'What about when it gets five or ten miles long and you have to walk five or ten miles out there just to start clearing and then you'll have to walk five or ten miles back? And what about when it gets to be fifteen miles? Or sixteen? Or—'

'I'll manage,' I said. I hadn't really thought about that potential problem, and I wished he hadn't mentioned it, because I would worry about it all day.

Ben said, 'Maybe you'll run into Uncle Nate up there. He's visiting his sweetheart.'

'Is not.'

'Is too, Zinny. That's what he said – "Guess I'll go see my sweetheart." '

'He's joking.'

'Is not.'

'Ben, have you seen Aunt Jessie – recently?'

'Yep.'

'Where? What was she doing?'

He poked at the dirt. 'Up by the barn, just walking.'

'She see you? She say anything?'

47

'Nope.'

'Maybe you imagined it,' I said.

'I did not imagine it.' He didn't seem at all bothered. In his nine-year-old mind, he thought it perfectly reasonable to see his dead aunt wandering through the farmyard.

I went on up to the trail, and as I cleared away weeds, I wondered if it were really possible to see a dead person, and felt terribly jealous that both Uncle Nate and Ben had seen her, but I hadn't. Maybe I hadn't looked hard enough. To be able to see her – oh! It gave me the shivers just thinking of it. To see her face, to see her walk in that funny way of hers – slow then fast, slow then fast – oh!

As I neared the barn on my way home, Ben joined me, and we saw Jake's truck leaving. 'Again?' Ben said. 'Wasn't he already here today?'

May, Gretchen, Bonnie, Will, and Sam were crowded around another cardboard carton – a big one this time, about a foot high.

'What is it, what is it, what is it?' Ben called.

May glared at me.

'Guess,' Bonnie said. 'It's from Jake.'

Inside the carton, squatting on loose hay, was a box turtle, about seven inches long. Its shell was high and round and black with eight orange splots. There was no sign of its head.

'Is it alive?' Ben asked.

'Jake said it was,' Gretchen said. 'He also said its name is Poke, and it's a weather predictor. If Poke keeps his head inside, it'll be good weather.

If Poke sticks his head out or scrabbles around, it's going to rain.'

'That doesn't make any sense,' Ben said. 'Wouldn't you think he'd rather stick his head out if the weather was good? And go inside when it rained?'

'I'm just telling you what Jake said, is all,' Gretchen said.

Just then, the turtle poked his head out, and as he did so, a raindrop splatted on his shell.

'Can I have it?' Ben asked, lifting it from the carton.

Bonnie said, 'Put it down. It's for Zinny.'

'Why for Zinny?'

'Because Jake said so.'

'But why for Zinny?'

May rolled her eyes. 'Probably because she collects all those stupid and immature things. He probably will bring over any old piece of rubbish he finds and give it to Zinny just to get rid of it. It's so embarrassing.'

That night the tree cricket chirped one hundred and twelve times in one minute. I divided that by four, and added thirty-seven, and it came out to sixty-five. I got out of bed and went down to the kitchen and checked the thermometer fastened to the outside of the window. The temperature was sixty-five degrees Fahrenheit.

I stared out the window at the oak tree. Beyond stretched dark shadows. Was Aunt Jessie out there? If I looked hard enough, long enough, would I see her?

12

The Birds, the Rose, and the Turtle

Every evening after dinner, Aunt Jessie and Uncle Nate used to swing slowly back and forth, back and forth, on the porch swing, gazing out at the ash tree and the rose garden in the front yard and at the river far in the distance. Railroad tracks ran alongside the river, and at six o'clock the mournful song of the train's whistle drifted through the valley.

Sometimes I sat with them on the swing. One evening, shortly after the train passed below, a male cardinal swooped to the ash tree. The brilliant red bird sat there a minute or two, looking around, as if he were waiting for someone, and then he plunged to the feeder which hung on a nearby branch. He snatched seeds, tapping them against the perch, breaking them open, and snipping out the soft insides with his beak. Seeds that didn't appeal to him were flung to the ground with a toss of his crested head.

'Where's his mate?' Uncle Nate asked. 'He's all by his lonesome. Poor old thing.'

After Aunt Jessie died, Uncle Nate sat alone on the swing. One night, from my upstairs window, I heard the train whistle below, softly, then louder, then fading into the distance. I saw a flutter of red as the male cardinal approached the tree and settled

50

in it. He sat there for several minutes looking around. And then – *there* – there she was, fluttering down beside him – a pale-brown female with red streaks on her head and wings.

The male flew to the feeder, selected a few seeds, and returned to the ash tree. He broke one open, snipped out the insides, and passed them to the female.

Uncle Nate stopped swinging. He leaned forward, watching. 'You lucky thing,' he said. 'You lucky old thing.'

At the sound of his voice, the female sprang from the branch and drifted across the yard toward a birch grove. The male waited behind in the ash tree until she had nearly disappeared from view, and then he plunged from the branch, swept close to the porch where Uncle Nate sat, and rose in the air to follow his mate.

'Lucky old thing,' Uncle Nate repeated.

Beyond the ash tree was a rose garden: twenty bushes planted by Uncle Nate the year that baby Rose died. Aunt Jessie loved those roses. She could see them from her bedroom window, and that summer, she and I would walk through them, counting the blooms.

When the first frost came in November, Aunt Jessie fretted. She stared out the window at the few remaining blossoms, stiff and matted with frost. 'They'll all die soon,' she said. It sent a shiver through me.

Each year after that, she was thrilled in the spring

when the first rosebud appeared, and each year, with the arrival of winter, she became dejected all over again, as if she didn't believe or didn't remember that spring would come again.

Several years after Uncle Nate had planted the roses, I was with my family one Saturday at a store in Chocton. Each of us kids had a dollar. The boys were sifting through the candy, May and Gretchen were at the make-up counter, and Bonnie and I were wandering around the store, unable to make up our minds what to choose. Then I saw it. It was perfect: a red plastic rose on a stiff green stem. I bought it and kept it in my closet until October, when I snuck it into the rosebushes in the yard, tying it to a branch.

When Aunt Jessie started to fret over the frost and the dying buds, I'd say, each morning, 'There's still a few left,' and, finally, 'There's still *one* left.' She didn't seem impressed and said, 'It'll be dead soon.'

By December, after we'd had two snowfalls, she could no longer ignore the single rose still blooming in the garden. On one of our walks, she headed for the bushes. 'I want to see this rose,' she said. I tried to discourage her, tried to pull her in another direction, but she was determined. She reached across the bush in front and touched my plastic rose.

'What?' she said, tugging at it. 'What . . .?' She pulled it loose, and the look on her face I'll never forget: such disappointment, such dismay. She threw the rose to the ground. 'It's fake! Who would do such a mean and nasty thing?'

My own face must have betrayed my guilt.

'You?' she said. 'You did that? How could you?'

I ran to the barn, ashamed and confused.

Later, she apologized, saying that she knew I hadn't meant to hurt her, that I must have thought it would please her. She didn't know why she had reacted the way she did. 'I so much wanted that rose to be *alive*,' she said.

Shortly afterward, she restored the red plastic rose to the rose garden, and it has bloomed there year round ever since, faded nearly to white, but still there. When Aunt Jessie died, Uncle Nate bought a second plastic rose and added it to the other one in the rose garden.

One day shortly after Jake had visited, I came around the side of the house and saw Uncle Nate sitting on the porch. I heard him say, 'Now whose little baby are you, sugar pie? Where's your mama? Ain't nobody keeping an eye on you, little darlin'?'

He was talking to Poke, the turtle, who was sitting in the middle of the porch.

'It's a turtle, Uncle Nate,' I said.

He leaned over and examined it. 'I knew it,' he said. 'Where's the other one?'

'What other one?'

'Don't be a noodle,' Uncle Nate said. 'This here turtle is all by his lonesome. He needs a mate. You tell Jake I said so.'

Two days later, Poke was missing, and Ben was frantic. 'The box is empty! Someone stole Poke!' He looked under bushes, trees, and the porch, as if Poke might have suddenly taken wing and flown out of the box.

I was under the porch trying to coax Ben out, when Uncle Nate thumped on the floorboards above us. 'What're you looking for down there?'

I scrabbled out. 'Poke. Ben thinks he might have—'

'Foot! That old turtle isn't under there.'

Ben crawled out from beneath the porch, brushing clumps of dirt from his shirt. 'He might be. He might be hiding—'

'Listen, tadpole,' Uncle Nate said. 'He ain't a-hiding. He's down at the creek this very minute searching . . .'

'For what?' Ben asked.

Uncle Nate thumped his stick firmly on the porch. 'For his sweetheart, that's what!'

Ben made me go with him to the creek to see if we could find Poke. We searched all along the bank, but didn't see any sign of him.

'How does Uncle Nate know Poke is down here anyway?' Ben asked.

'Maybe he brought him here.'

On the way back to the house, I found a cricket, which I took to the tree outside my bedroom window. I didn't see the one Jake had put there, but I figured it was around somewhere, because I'd heard it each night.

Mom called from an upstairs window. 'Bonnie? Zinny? Is that you, Zinny? Have you seen Uncle Nate?'

'A while ago, on the porch.'

'Go see what he's up to, will you?'

Uncle Nate wasn't on the porch or up at the barn.

Dad was in the field, weeding the tomato patch. 'Seen Uncle Nate?' I asked.

'Not lately.' He stood and looked around. 'Wait a minute – there he goes—'

Cresting the hill and waving his stick at our invisible Aunt Jessie was Uncle Nate calling, 'Wait on up! Wait on up!'

'Follow him, would you?' Dad said. 'Make sure he doesn't hurt himself.'

Uncle Nate ran down the hill, around the barn, through the squirt gardens, and around the house, circling the ash tree twice. Ben and I caught up with him as he started down the drive.

'Come on!' he shouted. 'Help me get her.'

We ran down the drive behind him. He had a funny, waddling gait, but he could run pretty fast. He turned and plunged into the bushes, where he was soon tangled and flailing. 'Dag-blasted branches!' He whacked his stick against the bush. 'Got away again.'

To Ben, I whispered, 'Did you see her?'

He nodded, his eyes wide open. 'Yep, I did, didn't you?'

I hadn't. *Why* couldn't I see her?

On our way back to the house, a truck crunched along the gravel drive behind us, and we stepped to one side as Jake pulled up. 'Hey!' he called. 'Get on in, and I'll give you a ride up to the house.'

'No thankee,' Uncle Nate said. 'Things to do.'

'Zinny? Ben?' Jake said.

'Have to keep an eye on him,' I said, watching my uncle cross the drive and head toward the ash tree.

Jake turned off the engine. 'I brought you something, Zinny.'

'Why?'

''Cause I like to.' He shoved a small brown paper sack at me.

Uncle Nate was off and running again. 'I've got to go after him.'

'Zinny – Zinny!' Jake called after me. 'Don't forget to open it. Hope you like 'em . . .' He drove up to the house, backed up, and turned around, leaving the way he had come.

Ben stood in the drive, yelling, 'Bring *me* something next time!'

'Zinny!' May called from the front door. 'Was that Jake?'

13

Bingo

Four smooth, white lucky stones were in the sack
Jake had given me. I slipped one stone into my pocket
and hid the rest upstairs in my closet. Bottle caps, a
cricket, a turtle, and lucky stones. These might sound
like innocent presents, and they were, but they were
the last of the innocent gifts.

The next day, he brought me a beagle puppy. It's
hard to resist a puppy.

'Do you like him?' Jake asked.

I stroked the puppy's back. 'Of course I like him.'
I handed him back to Jake. 'But I can't keep him.'

'What? Sure you can. He's yours.'

'Why? Why for *me*? Why not for someone else?'

Jake looked down at his feet. 'I know I'm older
than you, Zinny—'

'Three whole *years* older,' I said.

'I know it, but – I just want you to have him, that's
all.' He jammed his hands in his pockets. 'You're a
hard nut to crack, Zinny Taylor.' With that, he
jumped off the porch and headed for his truck.

'Take it back!' I shouted. I'm not sure whether I
meant the puppy or what he said about my being a
hard nut to crack. Maybe it was both. You might
think that I would've been convinced by this puppy,

that I'd believe that Jake really did like me and not
May. But I wasn't convinced. Tommy Salami had
gone on giving me gifts for a long, long time. So
had the others. You couldn't trust boys, I had
decided, no matter how nice they seemed, no matter
how many gifts they shoved into your hands, no
matter what they said. I guess you could say my
mind was pretty much made up about Jake Boone
and what he was up to.

May was fit to be tied. 'What'd he go and give you
a *dog* for? What in the world are you up to, Zinny?
Are you out of your ever-loving mind? You don't
have a lick of sense, Zinny. What you know would
fit in a nutshell.' She yanked all her ribbons off her
dresser and threw them on the floor. She was really
piling on the agony.

'Don't see what you're having such a conniption
about,' I said. 'I didn't *ask* Jake to bring me these
things . . .'

May gathered up the ribbons. 'Who said anything
about Jake?'

'You did – didn't you?'

'I never.' She threw the ribbons back on the floor
and looked wildly around the room. I thought she
was going to blow a gasket. 'Look at that bed of
yours – why, look at it! Why can't you make up your
bed like a normal human being?'

At dinner, all anyone could talk about was the puppy,
who was curled up on an old blanket in a corner of
the kitchen. Everyone took turns jumping up to see

if he was OK. We hadn't had a dog for two years, not since our last one was hit by a truck. Dad said he didn't mind having a dog around, but he wanted to know who was going to take care of it. Ben, Will, Sam, Gretchen, and Bonnie all assured him that they would.

'What about you, Zinny?' he asked. 'From what I can gather, this dog belongs to you.'

May said, 'I don't think we should have a dog. It'll just chew up everything. It'll get into my stuff, I know it will.'

'Fine,' I said. 'I'll give it back.'

'No, no, no!' My brothers wouldn't hear of it. They fell all over themselves promising to take care of it.

That night, after my sisters were asleep, I crept down to the kitchen and rescued the puppy from his lonely corner. I took him back to bed with me, petted him until he fell asleep, and gave him a name: Bingo. The name reminded me of Aunt Jessie leaning down to pick up her *wonders* and saying, 'Bingo!'

Two days later, when I was in Mrs Flint's store, I asked her if she had any specials.

'What do you mean, "specials"?' she said.

'You know, special prices – or a free bag of cookies—'

'Well, doesn't that beat all creation!' she said. 'A free bag of cookies! I'm trying to make a living here – which one are you?'

'Zinny.'

'I'm trying to make a living here, Zinny. Free bag of cookies! Whatever next . . .?'

On my way out, I saw this sign on the notice board:

LOST: 2-MONTH-OLD BEAGLE PUPPY. ANSWERS TO NAME OF GOBBLER. PLEASE PHONE 266–3554. ASK FOR BILL BUTLER. HIDDLE FARM, MORLEY ROAD, JUST PAST THE METHODIST CHURCH.

When I got home, the puppy was sleeping on the blanket in the kitchen. 'Gobbler,' I called. 'Gobbler . . .' His ears perked up, his eyes opened, and he ran toward me.

14

Gobbler

By mid-May, the days were getting longer, but I had less time to work on my trail. It was harder to get up there after school because the cleared section of the trail was nearly two miles long, and by the time I got up to where I had left off, it was time to turn back for supper. I couldn't wait for school to be out in three weeks, so I could make some headway on my trail. I was getting frantic, afraid that I'd never be able to finish it, and I'd be doomed.

The tomato plants had taken hold in the field and in our squirt gardens, and I'd crushed up eggshells to surround my plants. That's what Aunt Jessie used to do to keep the slugs and snails away. When the aphids came, I boiled up Aunt Jessie's secret brew: mashed-up marigolds, cigarettes (you could always find a few butts behind the barn where Uncle Nate would sneak his smokes), and onion skins, all boiled up into a stinking brew and sprayed on the plants.

I'd seen Poke twice at the creek, and he wasn't alone. He'd found a mate, and the two of them often sunned on an old log. Once Ben and I saw Uncle Nate down by the creek, digging for worms. 'Going fishing?' Ben asked him.

'Maybe so.'

Later, we saw Poke and his mate sitting on the log, feasting on that fresh pile of worms.

Dad once told me that when May was a toddler, someone had given her a turtle. She tired of it after a few weeks, but Aunt Jessie took a shine to it, feeding it raspberries and worms. As winter neared and the turtle stopped eating, Aunt Jessie put it in a box in her closet, and the following spring she brought it out again.

'Was it alive?' I asked.

'Sure it was. Alive and raring to go.'

'What happened to it?'

'She decided it was lonely and took it down to the creek.'

'Did she visit it?' I asked.

'Nearly every day. She took it raspberries and worms.'

The cricket had made its home on the tree outside my bedroom window, and nearly every night it told me the temperature. And the puppy . . . well, the puppy was gone.

The day after I'd seen the notice on Mrs Flint's bulletin board, Bingo and I went for a walk. By the time we got to Bybanks, his fur was matted with briars and leaves, his paws caked with mud, and his nose swollen from a bee sting. When I saw Jake's truck parked at Mrs Flint's store, we took a detour across the field, over the creek and back to the road. By this time, I was carrying Bingo, who had run out of steam and was looking bedraggled. He slept in my arms as we passed the Methodist church and headed up Morley Road.

I'd been to the Hiddle Farm so many times when Sal lived there that I could've walked there blindfolded. I'd only met the new renters, the Butlers, once. Bill Butler, who worked with my dad at the county airport, was a nice man, and I'd say most people liked him and his wife pretty well, but his mother – Old Mrs Butler, as she was known – was definitely off her rocker.

Old Mrs Butler thought she was six years old. She wore blue ribbons in her hair and a little yellow sunbonnet that didn't fit and sat like a crumpled handkerchief on top of her head. Her hair ran all the way down her back like thin gray rat tails. My dad and I found her one day playing in a mud hole behind the gas station, and we took her home. That was the only time I'd been to the Hiddle Farm since Sal left.

Now, as I walked along Morley Road, I got cold feet. I didn't want to take the puppy back. He was curled up in my arms so peacefully, nuzzling his nose up my sleeve. He was so much like a dog Sal used to have, Moody Blue. I sat down beneath a maple tree to think this over.

Maybe this wasn't the missing beagle. Maybe his name wasn't really Gobbler – although he leaped to that name each time I'd tried it on him. Finally, I decided I had to find out if Bingo was Gobbler, and I went up the road to Hiddle Farm, and all the way up the road I kept expecting to see Sal running toward me.

Old Mrs Butler was sitting on the side porch,

stringing beans. She wore her scrunched bonnet and blue ribbons. At her feet was a grown-up beagle, who leaped up and howled. Bingo woke with a start and squiggled from my arms, falling clumsily to my feet. Bingo sniffed once, howled in answer, and took off.

The two dogs met each other in the yard. The older one sniffed Bingo protectively, and Bingo leaped up, nuzzling her. Old Mrs Butler clapped her hands, squealed, grabbed a broom, and headed toward me. 'Shoo, shoo,' she said, waving her broom. She wasn't shooing the dogs. She was talking to me. 'Go on. Shoo. Get away . . .'

Old Mrs Butler let out a high-pitched giggle, an awful, frightening sound if ever I heard one. It sounded like the whinny of a mad horse. 'Gobbler, Gobbler, my Gobbler,' she called. Bingo ran straight for her and jumped against her legs, pawing at her thick stockings, which had been rolled down to her ankles.

I tried to explain who I was, but she kept swishing her broom at me. Then I decided maybe it was better if she *didn't* know who I was, so I said I'd heard they'd lost a puppy and this one had appeared at our house. It wasn't a complete lie. I just didn't mention *how* it had appeared or who had brought it.

'Shoo, go on, get away—'

'But is it *yours*?' I asked. 'Is this the dog you lost?' It was a needless question. From the way Bingo was behaving, it was obvious that he had come home and was as happy as could be.

'*Lost*?' Old Mrs Butler said. 'Get on out of here.

Shoo – you *thief*.' She chased me down the drive, and as I ran off down the road I could hear that terrible whinnying giggle.

At home, Ben was already in a fit. 'Zinny, where's Bingo? Have you seen him? He's gone!'

I wanted to tell the truth, I really did, but I didn't want to get Jake in trouble. If he had stolen that dog, and it certainly seemed he had, I didn't want anyone to know it. I didn't know if I was trying to protect Jake or save myself from a load of embarrassment. 'I took Bingo for a walk,' I said.

Will grabbed my arm. 'Then where is he?'

'Got loose . . .'

They were beside themselves. 'Then let's go after him! Where did he get loose?' They formed a search party and made me show them where I'd lost Bingo.

I led them down the drive and turned in the opposite direction from the way I'd gone with Bingo. About a hundred yards down the road, I stopped. 'He went through that thicket there – I've already looked. I searched and searched . . .' It was awful to lie. I hated it. But more than hating the lie, I was beginning to hate Jake for bringing the puppy in the first place. We looked for a long time, but of course there was no sign of Bingo, and we returned home, a sad, disappointed group.

I was desperate to get back to my trail, but at home everything was a mess. All through dinner that night, Bonnie, Gretchen, Will, Sam, and Ben moaned and whined and nearly drove me out of my mind about poor lost Bingo. Dad said, 'Zinny? I haven't heard too much from you about this. It was *your* dog, after all. You don't seem very upset.'

Ben said, 'Didn't you like him, Zinny?'

'Sure did. Sure, I'm upset.' I tried to show it. I frowned, sniffled, and looked as forlorn as a half-dead mule. I was pretty sure I was going to get zapped by lightning, too, for continuing this lie. I wanted to blurt out the truth, but I couldn't.

'Well, shoot a bug!' Uncle Nate said. 'Then go and *get* the dag-blasted dog! Don't just sit here twiddling your thumbs.'

Dad suggested I put up a lost-dog notice in Mrs Flint's store, and Bonnie said, 'Maybe you should call Jake—'

'What for?' I asked, my heart thudding in my chest.

'He'd help,' Bonnie said. 'I know he would—'

'Don't anybody tell Jake yet, OK?' I said.

'Why not?'

Mom said, 'Maybe Zinny doesn't want him to know she lost his present. Right, Zinny?'

'Right,' I said. 'That's it.' I wanted to crawl under the porch and stay there for a year or two.

All that evening, they pelted me with questions. Had I done the notice yet? Did I want any help? In the midst of this, Bonnie said, 'Wait a minute! If Zinny puts up that notice at Mrs Flint's store, then Jake will see it because he works there, and Zinny doesn't want Jake to know . . .'

I could have kissed her. Instead, I had to pretend that this was a puzzling problem. '*Now* what can I do?' I wailed. 'I can't put the sign up at Mrs Flint's – darn, darn, darn.' I felt such plunking relief, but found that it was almost too easy to pretend the opposite. *Zinnia Taylor: professional liar.*

My relief didn't last long, because everyone quickly decided that I would have to tell Jake. I *owed* it to him, they insisted. He would understand, they said. Gretchen was firm about it. 'It's settled. You put the sign up tomorrow and then tell Jake. He'll want to help us find Bingo.'

I made a quick decision. I'd make a sign and *pretend* to take it to Mrs Flint's. 'Here,' I said, dashing off a notice. 'How's this?'

LOST: BEAGLE PUPPY. ANSWERS TO NAME OF
BINGO. PLEASE PHONE Z. TAYLOR.

'You forgot to put our phone number on there,' Gretchen said. 'And the address. Here, I'll do it.' She sat down at the computer and spent an hour devising a sign which was, in my opinion, too bold and too prominent. 'There!' she said. 'Much, much better!'

15

Lost and Found

The next day was Saturday, and after breakfast I slipped out of the house. 'I'm going to Mrs Flint's to put up the notice,' I called behind me.

'Zinny! Wait!' Bonnie shouted. 'Mom needs some milk. She gave me the money—'

'OK, I'll get it.'

'I'll come with you,' she said.

I nearly choked. 'I can do it, Bonnie.'

'I *know* you can do it, Zinny. Don't be a goof. I just want to come, that's all.'

My brain was galloping as Bonnie chattered. 'Maybe Bingo is sniffing his way home right now. Dogs can do that, you know. I heard about a family who gave away their dog before they moved all the way across the country, two thousand miles, and do you know what that dog did, Zinny?'

I had a pretty good idea of what that dog did, but I wasn't in the mood for guessing.

'That dog followed that family's trail all the way across the country. Two thousand miles! Isn't that amazing? How do you think it did that, Zinny? I bet some of the family's smell was on the car and the dog sniffed his way along. At least Bingo won't have that far to sniff. Maybe he's sniffing his way home right now, don't you think, Zinny?'

I was relieved to see that Jake's truck was not at Mrs Flint's store. 'Bonnie, you get the milk and I'll put the notice up. I'm in a hurry to get back,' I said.

'And which one are you?' Mrs Flint asked Bonnie.

'I'm Bonnie. And that one is Zinny. She's putting up a notice on your board. Is that OK? Do we have to pay to do that?'

'No, it's a perfectly free service,' Mrs Flint said.

I tacked the notice to the board so that it was partially hidden by another one.

'Do you want to know what we're putting the notice up for?' Bonnie said to Mrs Flint. 'Zinny is very upset. She's lost her dog.'

I could have strangled her.

'What a shame,' Mrs Flint said.

'It's a little beagle puppy and his name is Bingo—'

'A beagle? My, my, everyone seems to be losing their beagles these days.'

I grabbed Bonnie's arm. 'Bonnie, *please*—'

'OK, OK, OK! I'm coming. You don't have to pinch me. I want to see the notice. Zinny! No one can see it *there*!' She removed it and replaced it front and centre. 'There – much better!'

'Bye, now,' Mrs Flint called. 'I hope you find your puppy.'

We were passing the school when Bill Butler drove by, honking his horn and waving at us. I turned back to see him pulling up in front of Mrs Flint's store. *Please, please, please*, I prayed, *do not let him see that notice.*

'Bonnie! I forgot something. You go ahead. I'll catch up.' I tore back to the store and dashed to the notice board.

Bill Butler turned from where he was standing at the counter with Mrs Flint. 'Hi there – which one are you . . .?'

'Zinny,' I mumbled, as I ripped the notice from the board.

'Are you taking your notice down?' Mrs Flint asked.

'Yes,' I said. 'We found what we were looking for.'

'Already?' Mrs Flint said. 'Aren't you the lucky one? And I understand you found your beagle, too, isn't that right, Bill?'

' "Too"?' he said.

'The Taylors lost a beagle, too, isn't that right, Zinny?'

I pretended I hadn't heard her and headed for the door just as Bonnie entered, saying, 'I almost forgot! Mom needs butter.'

I slapped the notice back on the board as Bonnie went in search of butter. *Please*, I prayed, *please do not let Mrs Flint or Bill Butler say anything to Bonnie about the 'newly found' puppy*. This one prayer, at least, was answered, for by the time Bonnie got to the counter, Mrs Flint was busy telling Bill about her gall bladder. She interrupted herself only once, as Bonnie left. 'Bye there, Bonnie, and I'm real happy for you . . .'

'Me, too,' Bill said.

As soon as we were out the door, Bonnie said, 'Why were they happy for me?'

'Must have you confused with someone else.'

'Maybe they found out I won the spelling contest,' Bonnie said.

'Probably . . .'

'How do you think they found out? Who do you think told them?'

I wasn't listening after that. All I could think about the rest of the way home was that notice sitting there on the board. What if Mrs Flint saw it – after she'd seen me take it down and after I'd told her we found the puppy? What if Bill Butler saw it? What if Jake saw it?

I was too miserable to think, and so I went up to the trail. For eight hours, I furiously pulled weeds and scraped stones. I plunged through nettles and thorns, pawing at the ground like a crazed badger. Two rain showers passed over me, soaking me to the skin, but I kept on going.

I found one clump of mushrooms and gobbled them down, hoping they were poisonous and that my punishment would be swift and violent. I'd probably feel dizzy, gag, throw up, tremble violently and fall dead right there on the path. My family would send out a search party. They'd find me there on my trail and they'd feel terrible. They'd wonder if I'd been murdered. They'd carry my pitiful body down the hill and clean me up and buy me a white dress and lay me in a quilted coffin surrounded by red zinnias. I hoped they wouldn't put me in the drawer.

They'd have a sweet service at the church and then take me to the cemetery. Jake would be there, weeping loudly. He'd say, 'It's all my fault. It's all my fault.' Then he'd tell everybody about stealing Bingo and how I had protected him. Everyone would say, 'Wasn't that Zinny the most noble thing on this earth?'

The mushrooms, however, were quite tasty, and I didn't die. I figured I'd have to go back to Mrs Flint's and retrieve that notice.

Too late, too late.

I was limping back down the trail and had just rounded the bend from where I could see our house below, when I spotted Jake's truck leaving. I crumpled in the grass. *Please do away with me now*, I prayed, *the quicker the better.*

'Zinny, Zinny,' Bonnie called. 'Guess who was here, and guess what he brought?'

'Don't tell me—'

'Jake! Jake was here and guess what he brought? He brought *Bingo* back! I knew he'd help. Jake saw the notice in the store and went out looking, and what do you know, he found him! Isn't that a miracle? Bingo was just walking along the road. Isn't that amazing? I bet he was sniffing his way back home, don't you think? Zinny? What's the matter, aren't you happy?'

'Zinny, guess what? You're late for school. Hurry up.'

I moved in slow motion, waiting for everyone else to leave for school and for Mom to take Uncle Nate's breakfast in to him. Then I scooped up my books and Bingo and set off. I'd be fiercely late for school, but I'd deal with that later.

I stopped at Mrs Flint's store and tied Bingo up outside. Mrs Flint was surprised to see me. 'Don't you have school?' she asked.

'I'm a little late,' I said, ripping my notice from the board.

'I thought you already took down your sign.'

'Had two of them up here. Forgot this one.'

'The funniest thing is that Mr Butler was just in here. He's lost his beagle again! Look there – he put up another notice.'

Sure enough, at the top of the board was a familiar sign:

LOST: 2-MONTH-OLD BEAGLE PUPPY, ANSWERS TO NAME OF GOBBLER. PLEASE PHONE 266-3554. ASK FOR BILL BUTLER. HIDDLE FARM. MORLEY ROAD. JUST PAST THE METHODIST CHURCH.

As soon as Mrs Flint turned her head, I ripped down his sign as well.

At the Hiddle Farm, I was once again greeted by the broom-waving Old Mrs Butler. Bingo-Gobbler howled, and the mother beagle responded with louder howls as she raced toward us. Over these howls came Old Mrs Butler's fearsome whinny, followed by, 'Gobbler, Gobbler, Gobbler!'

I dropped Bingo and was out of there so fast I split the breeze. As I tore past the high school which May and Gretchen – and Jake – attended, I was steaming. I halted in my tracks, tore a sheet of paper out of my science book and wrote on it. Inside, I handed it to the secretary. 'You must be a Taylor,' she said. 'Which one—'

I lied. 'Bonnie. Could you please see that Jake Boone gets that? It's important. It's from his mother.'

I headed lickety split for the middle school, a block away. I sure hoped the secretary wouldn't read the note. I had written:

IF YOU BRING THAT DOG BACK AGAIN,
I'LL PUNCH YOUR BRAINS OUT.

I had signed it 'Z.T.' I wanted Jake to know exactly who he was dealing with.

16
Boogie-woogie

Even before I went in the house, I heard the music. It was that wild, crazy jiving beat of the boogie-woogie that I hadn't heard since Aunt Jessie died. She and Uncle Nate had played their favourite boogie-woogie record on special occasions: their anniversary, their birthdays. They'd dance up a storm to this music, twirling and wiggling and spinning to beat the band. It was so unlike the quiet, gentle way they usually were.

Aunt Jessie would laugh her head off, her red hair bobbing and the fat on her arms jiggling. Uncle Nate adopted a serious look when he was dancing, as if he were in a contest and didn't want to mess up, but when the record stopped, he put his hands on his knees and laughed – how he laughed and laughed, until tears rolled down his cheeks.

They sure loved that boogie-woogie. They even had this thing they'd say to each other, from *The Boogie-woogie Bugle Boy* song. If Uncle Nate was leaving the house, he'd say, *Tootle-ee-ah-dah!* And Aunt Jessie would say, *Make the company jump!* They'd do this all the time. *Tootle-ee-ah-dah! Make the company jump!*

*

As I came in the house this time, I realized I hadn't heard Uncle Nate say *Tootle-ee-ah-dah* lately, either. Hearing that music again made me feel so pitiful I could hardly stand it.

I went through the kitchen passage and down the hall to Uncle Nate's room, where the record player was blaring away. His door was slightly ajar. Inside, he was dancing like a wild man with an invisible partner.

17

Trespassing

For a week, there was no sign of Jake. May asked me if I'd said anything to make him mad, because he was ignoring her at school. 'He won't even look at me,' she said. 'What'd you do, Zinny?'

'Not a ding-busted thing,' I said.

Everyone else was heartbroken over the lost-again Bingo. We had several searches, and they made me put up another notice (which I promptly took back down) at Mrs Flint's store. Bill Butler stopped me one day as I was walking to school and said his puppy was back, but he'd heard ours was missing again. He was sure sorry about that. He wished he could give us his, but his mother was too attached to it.

Bonnie kept insisting that Bingo was probably sniffing his way home that very minute, and every morning and evening, she'd stand out in the yard and call him.

One Saturday, I was up on the trail, clearing the part where it entered the first section of woods, marked on one of the maps as Maiden's Walk. Ahead of me was a tunnel of beech trees. Overhead hung a roof of branches and leaves, and below, the smooth grey-blue trunks looked like a double row of columns stretching into the forest. It was a silent, eerie, cool place, dark as a wolf's mouth.

When I had first seen the words *Maiden's Walk* on the map, I'd imagined a young woman, dressed in white, gliding down a sunny lane. Now, seeing what was ahead of me, I pictured a dishevelled maiden, in torn clothing, being pulled toward a horrid sacrifice. I saw her struggling and screaming, and glimpsed the drooling jaws of a black beast at the far end of the tunnel.

I was down on my hands and knees, scraping away, trying to rid my mind of this picture. *And now the company jumps*, I sang, to the beat of the boogie-woogie. *A-toot a-toot—*

I thought I heard a whistle. No. It was quiet. *A-tootle-ee-ah-dah—* I heard the muffled whistle again and froze, still as a stone.

The whistler was approaching. I inched behind a beech tree and scrunched myself into a ball at its trunk. Soon the whistling stopped, but it was followed by another sound – a *tap-tap-tapping* against the ground, as if someone were swinging a stick.

It was probably Uncle Nate, I thought, looking for Aunt Jessie. Or maybe he was meeting someone. Maybe he really did have a sweetheart up here in the hills. I hated that thought. He'd better *not* have a sweetheart.

As I started toward the sound of the stick, a tall figure appeared at the entrance to the woods. With the sun behind him, all I could see was a dark form and a long crooked stick. It wasn't Uncle Nate. I turned and ran, tall-stepping over uncleared brambles, scrabbling and tearing at branches.

'Zinny, Zinny! Wait!'

I kept running. I knew the voice and I didn't want to see its owner.

'Zinny . . .' He lurched up behind me and snagged my arm.

'Let go of me, Jake Boone, or I'll—'

'Punch my brains in?' He looked as solemn as a drowned man.

I pulled my arm free. 'What are you doing up here? How'd you know where I was?'

'Heck, Zinny, there's a dad-burn trail leading right to you—'

'But it's *my* trail. You get off it.'

He looked down at his feet. We were standing in a patch of dead leaves and weeds, a good distance from the cleared section of the trail.

'This?' he said. 'This doesn't look like a trail to me—'

'You know what I mean. Get out of here. This is mine . . .'

'You own all this? You, Zinny Taylor—?'

'Go away.'

He blushed and swung his stick and jabbed his foot at the leaves. 'Zinny, I'm sorry about the dog . . .'

'You oughta be. Stealing an old lady's innocent puppy—'

'I didn't actually steal it. It followed me – the first time, anyway. After I'd made a delivery up there. It chased my truck, so I stopped and picked it up, and – I don't know – I just wanted you to have it.'

I stood there, trying to keep the steam from coming out of my ears. 'And the second time?'

He stared at the ground. 'I saw your sign and I went back and snuck him into my truck. I couldn't help it.'

'Of course you could help it,' I said. 'Did someone hold a knife to your throat and say, "Take this dog or else?" ' I started walking back the way I'd come.

'You're enough to make the parson swear, Zinny, and I mean it.' He took ahold of my arm again. 'Didn't anyone ever like you before?'

'Let go – of course people have liked me – they like me all the time – lots and lots of—' I was stunned. What did he mean, 'before'?

'Name one—'

'Are you crazy? I have friends—'

'Not like that. I mean has anyone ever been sweet on you?'

Oh sure, I wanted to say. *Tommy Salami and Jerry Abbott and Mickey Torke – all those lying, phony boys*. I don't know what came over me. With my free hand I punched him in the chest and called him *a stupid worm*. Not exactly the height of sophistication, I suppose.

I guess I caught him off guard. He reached in his pocket, pulled out a little box, forced it into my hand, and stomped off. I threw the box after him. 'I don't want it. Take it back . . .'

He marched through the woods until he came to the clearing, where he turned down the trail toward our farm.

I swore every cuss word in the book and some new ones I made up. Then I went looking for the box. It seemed a shame not to at least see what was in it.

18

Proof

I'd no sooner walked in the house than Uncle Nate stumbled in behind me. His hair was all mussed up, and briars stuck to his shirt and pants. In one hand was his stick, and in the other hand he waved his camera. 'I've got it, I've got it!' he shouted.

'Got what?' I asked.

'The proof!' He gently set the camera on the table. 'Right in there,' he said, tapping the camera. 'Can't get away.'

By this time, everyone else had crowded around. 'What's in there?' Ben asked. 'What sort of proof?'

'Is it a picture, you mean?' Bonnie said.

'Of course it's a picture,' May said. 'You don't think he's gone and stuck a sack of potatoes in there, do you?'

Ben placed his hand on Uncle Nate's shoulder. 'Why is it proof, Uncle Nate? What's it a picture of?'

Uncle Nate glanced at each of us before whispering, 'My Redbird.'

Ben's eyes nearly popped out of his head. 'Aunt Jessie? You've taken a picture of her?'

Uncle Nate tapped the camera again. 'I've seen her. I've got proof.'

19

Accused

I had searched a long time for the box I'd thrown at Jake and finally discovered it tangled in a raspberry bush. It was a small silk-covered black box, with a rounded top and a tiny gold hinge at the back. I held the box out in front of me and opened it a wee bit, ready to snap it shut in case something ghastly was lurking inside. First I saw a glimpse of white silk. Nothing moving yet. I opened it wider.

Nestled in a slim groove in the centre of the white silk was a ring. A round red gem sat between two sparkling clear ones on a thin gold band. It fitted me.

Quickly, I slipped the ring back in the box. No one had ever given me anything like that before. In fact, no one had ever given me any jewellery whatsoever, except for the plastic ring from Tommy Salami. What was Jake Boone up to? I think this was the first time I thought I might have had Jake all wrong. *Was* it possible that Jake was not like Tommy Salami and all those others? I really wanted to believe that this ring was meant for me, and it was given to me because Jake liked me. I really, really wanted to believe that. But if he did like me, *why* did he like me? Why didn't he prefer May?

And then my mind got all mixed up. What was I supposed to do? And how did I feel about Jake? I hated being confused. I liked to know what was what.

I went on down the trail until I came to the place where I'd found the leather pouch buried under a stone. I slid the stone aside and dropped the ring in its box into the hole. When I was scooping dirt over it, I had that awful, chilling feeling again. There was something about this place. What *was* it?

I needed time to think, but what I started thinking about was Aunt Jessie.

The day after Aunt Jessie was buried, I remembered the leather pouch with the TNWM medallion, and went searching for it in the barn, but I couldn't find it. Had she scooped it back up again, or had someone else picked it up?

At dinner the day after the funeral, I had asked if anyone had seen an old pouch with a 'sort of medal-thingy' inside. I tried to make light of it, so that whoever had it might be more willing to confess. No one admitted finding it, though. Dad said, 'Ask Nate, maybe he's seen it.'

'Where *is* he anyway?' Ben had asked.

'Off on one of his treks,' Dad said. He and my mother exchanged a glance – troubled and annoyed.

'He's too old to be up there,' my mother said.

Dad grunted. 'You try and stop him.'

I had a feeling they knew something that I didn't. While Uncle Nate was off on his trek, I snuck into his and Aunt Jessie's house, figuring I'd just have a quick look.

It was awful being there without Aunt Jessie. Some of her things were gone: her coat no longer hung on the back of the door; her slippers weren't curled beside the sofa; and her knitting basket wasn't by her chair. That big dresser drawer was back in its place, though, and I wanted desperately to open it, having the sudden feeling that maybe she was hiding in it, but I couldn't do it.

I checked the bathroom last. This was Aunt Jessie's pride and joy, her new bathroom, finished a few months earlier. She'd always wanted a pink bathroom, and finally she got one, and it certainly was pink: pink tub, pink sink, pink carpet, pink towels, pink toilet paper. Uncle Nate started slipping into our house to use the bathroom. 'Pink makes me kind of queasy,' he said.

Beneath the sink were three drawers, and one of them, by Aunt Jessie's request, had a lock on it. I couldn't imagine what she'd want to keep locked up in the bathroom, but she had made Uncle Nate go to a lot of trouble to fit a locked drawer in that cabinet. I tried the drawer. Definitely locked. I thought about searching for a key, but was instantly ashamed, and instead I wiped off the sink and polished the taps, just as she had liked them.

Somebody had that medallion and sooner or later I was going to find out who. *Zinnia Taylor: detective*.

A week after Jake gave me the ring, Uncle Nate's film arrived. We all crowded around as he opened the packet, eager to see his 'proof'. One by one, he turned over the pictures: our cows, the barn, the ash tree, the cardinals.

'Where is it?' Ben asked. 'Hurry up.'

Slowly, Uncle Nate went through the pictures. 'That ain't it,' he said. 'That ain't it, either.' On he went: the porch, the field of tomatoes, Poke at the creek. As he turned over the picture of Poke, he shouted, 'There! There it is!' He looked up at us, excited, eager, proud, and expectant.

'There's what?' Ben asked.

'The proof, dag-blast it, the proof!' The photo was blurry, as if taken during an early-morning mist.

'Nate,' Mom said gently. 'It's a picture of *you* . . .'

'Where's the proof?' Ben asked.

'Right there before your eyes,' Uncle Nate said.

'But it's *you*—' Mom repeated.

'I know *that*. I ain't a complete noodle.'

'But where's the *proof*?' Ben pleaded. 'Where's Jessie?'

Uncle Nate grinned. 'Dag-blast it, *she* took the picture!'

In the midst of the hush which followed Uncle Nate's announcement, Mrs Boone arrived. I'd not seen her for years and years, and I wouldn't have known who it was if Mom hadn't greeted her at the door. The Mrs Boone I remembered was a plump, hearty woman with soft brown hair. This new version of Mrs Boone – or Louanne, as my mother knew her – was a skinny, frail thing with hair like stiff straw. Her chicken neck stretched forward, supporting a face lined with wrinkles. It was as if someone had opened up the former Mrs Boone and released the one inside – and the one inside wasn't a little girl – it was a little old lady.

I couldn't take my eyes off her, trying to figure out if maybe this was a different Mrs Boone. But my mother acted as if there was nothing whatsoever that was different about her – except that she seemed upset.

'Sit yourself down, Louanne,' my mother said. 'You look frazzled.'

'I am,' she said, darting a glance at us kids who were still gathered around Uncle Nate and his photographs.

'Why don't you all go in tne other room so Louanne and I can talk?' my mother said.

'Maybe one of them should stay,' Louanne said.

It was a peculiar thing for her to say, and we all stared at her, waiting for her to explain.

'Which one's Zinny?' she said.

Gretchen pushed me forward. 'This one.'

'Maybe Zinny should stay,' Louanne said. 'What I've got to say concerns her.'

I thought about bolting for the door and making a quick escape, or falling down in a fit and thrashing around and maybe even going unconscious. Everyone hovered there, curious about why Louanne Boone wanted me to stay.

'Go on,' Mom said, 'go find something to do. Zinny – you stay here.'

Reluctantly, they shuffled out of the room – all, that is, except May, who decided to wash the dishes.

'May, you too. Go on.'

'I'll just do up these dishes first,' she said.

'Go *on*—'

'OK, OK, OK! If you don't want any help, that's perfectly fine with me!' May said, stomping off.

Mrs Boone fiddled with her keyring, clearing her throat several times. 'You got new curtains,' she said.

'Three years ago,' Mom said.

'And I like the way you're doing your hair.'

'Thank you, Louanne. Yours looks nice, too.' (It didn't, though. Mom was just being polite.) 'Now, is there some reason you wanted Zinny to be here?'

Mrs Boone wouldn't look at me, so I was real worried. She said, 'I hope I'm wrong about this. I hate to do this.'

'What, Louanne? What is it? Does it concern Zinny?' Mom glanced from Mrs Boone to me. 'Zinny, have you any idea—?'

'Nope,' I said, which wasn't exactly the up-and-down truth, because I knew it had something to do with Jake. Maybe Mrs Boone knew about the puppy and thought it was my fault.

'Louanne . . .? Tell us what's bothering you,' Mom said.

'OK then, I will, but I don't like to do it. You know I don't usually do things like this. You know that usually I let things roll right off me. I don't complain. I don't meddle around in other people's business. But this is different.'

Just spit it out! I wanted to say. *Tell me the awful horrible thing I've done and hang me from the oak tree. Get it over with!*

'My Jake mentions Zinny all the time . . .'

I believe I turned purple when she said this.

'That's nice – isn't it?' Mom said. 'Does he ever mention May?'

Ah, I thought. Even Mom suspected he'd be more interested in May. Nobody would love *me*. I was mortified that she was announcing it like this.

Louanne twisted our tablecloth in her hands. 'Well, yes, he does. Maybe I've got them confused. I thought Zinny was the older one. Maybe you oughta call May back in here.'

Mom summoned May, who must have been inches away from the door, because she reappeared instantly. 'Yes?' she said brightly.

Louanne pressed her lips tightly together and gave the tablecloth a few more twists. Then she sat there, rigid as a fence post. Silent. The second hand on our clock flicked its way mercilessly toward the next second, and the next, and the next. I was beginning to think maybe she'd had a heart attack.

When she finally spoke again, I flinched.

'I was cleaning out my dresser drawers today. In the top drawer, under my stockings, I keep a little box with my valuables in it. I don't have too many valuables, just a few things my grandmother gave me. And pretty regularly, I take out this box and look at those things. It makes me feel good. I like to touch them.'

A flicker of recognition flipped around the edges of my brain.

'And today when I looked in that box, I knew right away that one was missing – my grandmother's

diamond and ruby engagement ring. I asked my
husband if he'd seen it. No, he hadn't. I would've
asked Jake, but he's been gone all morning, and he's
not at Mrs Flint's. I have a hunch he took my ring
and gave it to May or Zinny. There, I've said it.'

I thought she should have waited to ask Jake about
it, but I guess she wasn't thinking straight. I guess
she got frantic.

May burst into tears, and I was out of my chair
and at the door. I felt trapped, cornered.

'Zinny?' Mom said. 'Where—'

I was off and running.

20

Beady Eyes

The sun was directly overhead, beating down as I ran up the trail. My heart was thudding and my feet were pounding, *thunk, thunk, thunk* on each stone. The birds must have thought it was too hot to fly, because they clustered in the treetops, chattering.

When I lifted the stone which marked the spot where I'd buried the ring, a pale-brown salamander raised its head and fixed its gaze on me. I must have looked like a big sweaty giant hovering overhead. This might sound strange, but it seemed as if that salamander was trying to tell me something. Before I could figure out what, the salamander darted under a patch of pine needles.

The ring was *gone*.

I didn't know what to think. I dug farther down and pawed at the pine needles all around the spot. I searched the surrounding trees and bushes, but found nothing, and on my way back down the hill, I kept seeing those little beady salamander eyes staring at me.

I burst through the kitchen door, ready to confess all. Mrs Boone was gone, but Mom was standing at the sink.

'Zinny? You look a wreck. There, there. I don't

blame you for rushing out. That was a horrid thing Louanne did. Imagine her suspecting her own son of stealing. I told her that Jake wouldn't do such a thing, and even if he did – *if* he did – neither you nor May would have accepted it, and you would have told us about it. Don't you worry. Everything will be OK.'

I was dumbfounded. My head was saying *Confess! Confess!*, but my pitiful heart was so grateful for her comfort that I couldn't speak. It was selfish of me, I knew it, but at the time, I wanted to believe that everything *would* be OK, as simply as that.

That night as I was brushing my teeth, I heard the music again. I walked outside and glanced into Uncle Nate's room. On his mirror he had taped the picture of himself – the 'proof'. Round and round the room he spun, doing the boogie-woogie.

There was something about that music and seeing Uncle Nate looking so determined as he spun around that made *me* determined. I was going to find that ring and that medallion, and figure out exactly what was going on.

21

Wanted

At last, school was out, and I could concentrate on my trail. There'd been no sign of Jake since Mrs Boone had visited, and May and Gretchen whispered endlessly at night.

'You notice Jake hasn't been around?' Gretchen said.

'Shh,' May said. 'Is Zinny asleep?'

I slowed my breathing and kept still.

'She's out cold,' Gretchen said. 'What about Jake?'

'I think he finally wised up. Can you keep a secret?'

'Of course I can.'

'I think he was just bringing Zinny things to make me jealous,' May said. 'And you know that thing about the ring . . .? Here's what I think. I think Jake *did* take that ring—'

'No!' Gretchen said.

The ring, the ring. It had been on my mind night and day. Maybe I only *thought* I'd buried it in that hole. Maybe I'd dropped it somewhere.

May whispered to Gretchen, 'Wait – I think he took it and he was going to give it to *me*, but then he . . . oh, I don't know. Maybe he chickened out. Maybe he lost it. But I definitely think he – promise not to tell?'

93

'Promise.'

'I definitely think he likes me.' May giggled. 'You know what he did yesterday? I was at Mrs Flint's store, and Jake was there, and he – well, it was *so* obvious . . .'

'What was?'

'You know, that he likes me,' May said. 'He smiled at me.'

'He does smile a lot,' Gretchen said.

'This was different. I could just tell.'

I buried my head under my pillow, cursing Jake.

One evening, when Dad and Ben were watching a baseball game on television, I overheard Ben say, 'Dad, how come Zinny's never home any more? How come she's always on the trail?'

'I guess she likes to be out on her own sometimes,' Dad said.

'Not sometimes, *all* the time!'

'She'll get tired of it, sooner or later.'

'But she's not nearly done. She's got miles and miles to go,' Ben whined.

'She'll get tired of it, you watch. She won't finish it.'

My own father, a *traitor*, I thought.

The trouble was, I was starting to panic. By my estimate, I'd cleared only four miles of the trail; there were sixteen more to go. I had to finish it in the summer – I *had* to – but I was beginning to think it was an impossible task.

It now took me more than an hour to get up there, and once I cleared farther, it would take longer and longer just to get to where I'd left off. I was doomed. Then I had an idea, and I put it to Mom and Dad one evening.

'Zinny, you must be out of your mind,' my father said.

'A horse!' my mother said. 'You might as well be asking for an airplane. We don't have that kind of money.'

'But,' I pleaded, 'then I could ride up the trail, and it wouldn't take me nearly so long, and—'

'Zinny,' Dad said, 'don't you think this trail thing is getting out of hand?'

'Trail *thing*? It's not a trail *thing*. It's *my* trail. Aunt Jessie would have let me have a horse.'

That was the wrong thing to say. My mother burst into tears, and my father gave me a scathing look. '*No horse*,' he said.

I was desperate, and so I did a desperate thing. I put up a notice in Mrs Flint's store:

WANTED: CHEAP HORSE. NEED DESPERATELY.
PLEASE PHONE Z. TAYLOR.

I didn't have any money for a horse, not even a cheap horse. The reason I put that sign up was because I hoped Jake would see it. I hoped he would bring me a horse, and I didn't care if he had to *steal* it.

22

The Fence

Nothing was going right. It was as if the world were in cahoots with my father, who thought I wouldn't finish the trail.

The very day I'd put the sign up at Mrs Flint's, I was clearing the trail and, after a few hours' work, noticed a brighter patch ahead. The tunnel of woods known as Maiden's Walk was coming to an end. Weary of being closed in among the dark trees, I stopped clearing and walked ahead through the dead branches and rotting leaves to see what I could look forward to in the days ahead.

As I came through the last bank of trees, I sucked in my breath. Stretching before me was a clearing, about two hundred feet across: a meadow of tall grass and wildflowers, and beyond, the forest continued. This meadow might have been a sweet sight, but it wasn't, for surrounding it was a sturdy barbed-wire fence.

A *fence*? On *my* trail? I surveyed the meadow. No sign of any animals: no cows or horses or goats. It didn't even occur to me to continue the trail *around* the meadow. I was sure the trail had originally continued straight on, and for some reason, it was important to stay on that track. I headed back, planning my strategy.

At home, Dad handed me a piece of paper. 'Zinny, what's the meaning of this?' It was the sign I'd put up at Mrs Flint's, advertising for a horse. 'Where do you expect to get the money to pay for this "cheap" horse?'

'I could earn it,' I said.

'How?'

'Doing jobs for people.'

'When?'

'Whenever . . .'

'So you'll give up working on the trail in order to do these jobs?'

I stuffed the paper in my pocket. 'No,' I said. 'No, I will not. Forget the stupid horse, then. I'll just wear out my stupid legs.'

All I could think of was that I hoped Jake had seen the sign before Dad removed it.

The next day, I rummaged through the toolshed, looking for a pair of wire cutters. It was a mess in there, with scythes, hoes, hatchets, and pitchforks tilting helter-skelter among cobwebbed planks. Strewn across the wooden bench were plastic tubs of nails, screws, nuts, and bolts; screwdrivers and pliers and hammers; empty oil cans and coffee cans; and tangled loops of twine. I rummaged through this hodgepodge, burrowing under piles of metal, sending several spiders and a stunned mouse scurrying.

Seeing the coffee cans reminded me of the one I'd

put the snake in. I shook a few of the cans, to see if any tools were stuffed inside. One can rattled and clanked. Inside were dozens of coins, or at least I thought they were coins, but when I dumped them out, I saw that they weren't real coins, but tokens. Large ones, small ones, silvery, brassy. Some were plain, and some had designs or lettering. There was a cow on one, a bird on another. One said *Lucky* and another said *Free*.

They reminded me of the medallion I'd found, but there were none exactly like the medallion. In the midst of sifting through them, I got that wretched chilling feeling again, a dark, foreboding sense of something terrible happening all around me. I stuffed the tokens back into the can, and shoved it back where I'd found it.

As I headed back up the trail, Uncle Nate's voice scared the living daylights out of me. I felt as if I'd been caught – but at what? I'd only taken the wire cutters. I'd bring them back.

'Hey!' he called. 'Don't like you being on that trail!'

'Why not?'

'Don't think you should be up there alone. Don't know what you'll run into. No place for a girl.'

That was the wrong thing for him to say. 'You mean it would be OK for a boy to be up there, but not me?'

He chewed on his lip. 'Snakes up there . . .'

'Haven't seen any – lately. Anything else up there I might run into?' And then, I don't know what made me say this, but I added, 'Anybody's sweetheart?'

'Shoot!' he said, but he blushed and pushed the toe of his boot into the dirt. 'Your Aunt Jessie wouldn't like you going up there, that's all.'

I had a strange reaction to this. I almost said, *So what?* which would have been a horrible thing to say, and which surely I didn't mean, did I? And then I almost said, *Yes, she would like it*, because it was beautiful up there, and she loved trees and flowers. I suddenly felt very small and alone, as if no one understood what I was doing or why it was important to me, and I was not able to explain it to them because *I* didn't know why it was so important to me.

Unable to answer him, I turned away and started up the hill. Behind me, Uncle Nate called, *Tootle-ee-ah-dah!* and instantly – without thinking – I answered, *Make the company jump!*

Then I stopped dead in my tracks, realizing what he'd said. Uncle Nate had never said *Tootle-ee-ah-dah* to anyone but Aunt Jessie. And as I continued up the trail, I kept thinking about my automatic answer, *Make the company jump!* I'd said it with the same hopeful, happy burst Aunt Jessie had always said it. What did that mean, *Make the company jump!*? I wasn't sure. The way Aunt Jessie said it made it sound as if the words meant, *Go to it!* or *Live! Live it up!*

And I wondered why – when Aunt Jessie had

climbed into her drawer – why I hadn't leaned down and said, *Make the company jump! Make the company jump!* Maybe if I'd said that, she would've climbed out of that drawer and started dancing.

23

Don't Blame Me

It's not easy to cut through barbed wire, even if you have a pair of heavy-duty wire cutters. Eventually, though, after twisting, pulling, kicking, and scolding, I managed to cut through four lengths of double-stranded wire and pull each length back to the posts. This was a terrible thing to do, to ruin a fence. I am a farm girl, and I know how long it takes to repair a fence. But that day, I was like a bull with his tail on fire. That fence was in my way and it had to go.

When I started scraping away at the ground, however, I couldn't find any stones – stones which should have continued the trail – beneath the grass. The stones stopped abruptly this side of the fence, and continued on the other side of the meadow, beyond that fence. Maybe someone had cleared this area of trees in order to make the meadow, and in doing so, they must have cleared the stones as well.

I wasn't sure what to do. I could just clear the grass, and this part of the trail would be simply dirt, but then the grass and weeds would quickly return and cover the trail. I could find some stones and lay them myself, but I needed large slate slabs, and the only place I knew I could find these was back at the creek. I'd be lucky if I could find enough. Then

I tried to picture myself trekking over four miles back to the creek, and lugging stones, a few at a time, four miles back. It didn't seem very practical, and it would take me ages.

I walked the length of the fence as it ran down the hill to the right, to see if there was a farmhouse near, but another meadow stretched far below. No sign of a house or barn.

When I turned back, a dark pile off to one side caught my eye. Dozens of cast-off slate slabs were heaped haphazardly. I'd still have to lug them back to where I'd cut the barbed wire, but I could probably do it in a day or two.

Clearing the tall grass, though, proved to be harder than I'd imagined. I was going to have to go back and fetch a scythe.

Ben was kneeling in the midst of his squirt garden, scolding newly sprouted weeds. My own garden was looking sad and neglected. The tomato plants, which I'd not staked well, leaned mournfully toward the ground, heavy with green tomatoes. Weeds tangled wilder than witches' hair. The zinnias around the border looked pitiful, cluttered with dead blooms and wilting from the bright sun.

Ben said, 'Your garden's a mess, Zinny. You oughta do something about it.'

'I will,' I said.

'Jake's been here. It wasn't me who got things wrong, Zinny. It was Sam.'

'Got *what* things wrong?'

'You'll see.'

In the kitchen, Bonnie took one look at me and blurted, 'Guess who's been here and guess what happened?'

Sam, who was standing at the counter slopping leftovers into a huge pot for his daily soup concoction said, 'Don't blame *me*, Zinny.'

'For *what*?'

Sam furiously stirred his mixture. 'I don't remember so good. I wasn't paying attention.'

Gretchen sauntered in, and seeing me, stopped short. 'Jake's been here. He brought something for May.'

'Maybe not,' Bonnie said. 'It might not have been for May—'

'It was—'

'Might not have been.'

Sam was stirring his soup like a madman. 'Don't blame *me*.'

Bonnie said, 'Jake was here, and he brought something, and Sam was the only one around, so he gave it to Sam, but Sam can't remember who Jake said to give it to.'

'I wasn't paying attention,' Sam whimpered.

'May says it's for her,' Gretchen said.

'Might not have been . . .'

I headed for the toolshed, with Bonnie close on my heels. 'Don't you want to know what it was?' she asked. 'Aren't you curious? Don't you think it was probably for you?'

I stopped. 'OK. What was it?'

Bonnie clutched my arm. 'A horse.'

24

The Horse

I raced up the hill to the barn, pushed open the
squeaky wooden door, and stood still, inhaling the
familiar smell of hay and manure. When my eyes
had adjusted to the darkness, I made my way down
to the stalls, listening for sounds of the new animal.

That wonderful Jake, I was thinking. *That blessed
Jake*.

The stalls were empty. In the pasture, I found only
our two cows munching methodically at the grass. I
turned and surveyed the rest of the farm. Bonnie was
climbing the hill toward me, and below, in the squirt
garden, Ben tended his beans.

'So where is it?' I asked Bonnie when she reached
me.

'Where's what?'

'The *horse*!'

Bonnie looked around. 'What horse?'

'Honestly, Bonnie – the horse Jake brought!'

'Oh Zinny, you goof,' she said. 'It's not a *real*
horse. It's a *wooden* horse.'

In the toolshed, I found the scythe and made my way
back up the trail. *That idiot Jake*, I cursed.

Furiously, I swung at the meadow grass with the

scythe. I was clumsy with the tool, nearly whacking my foot off several times, but eventually I got into a rhythm, and then it was as if my mind and body and the scythe and the grass were all connected. I swished my way across the meadow, surprised when I came to the fence on the other side that I was finished already and still had both my feet. I cut the barbed wire on the far side of the fence and lugged stones from the pile further below.

What was happening to me? Why did I hope Jake would *steal* something for me? Normally I thought stealing was awful. Maybe I was looking for proof that he liked me. That was an ugly thing to consider, that I'd expect someone to do something so awful just to prove he liked me. I felt like a little kid demanding candy: *I want it! I want it now!* Only I didn't want candy; I wanted a horse, and I wanted to know who Jake really liked. In my mind I could hear May saying, *Oh, Zinny, you're so immature!*

In bed that night, I listened to the tree cricket. It was seventy degrees outside, and a warm breeze teased the curtains. On May's bedside table across the room was a small brown box, and beside it stood a minia-ture wooden horse.

The horse *had* to be meant for me, and I was tempted to snatch it from the table. Jake *was* giving these things to me, for me, wasn't he? But then I wondered why May was so *sure* it was for her, and if Jake had said something, and if he had changed his mind.

My dreams that night were filled with bizarre

images. Gold medallions and ruby rings shimmered in the trees, and brass tokens fluttered in the air. Racing through the woods were tiny brown horses chasing beagles and beady-eyed salamanders. In the midst of all this, my Aunt Jessie danced on the trail, doing the boogie-woogie, while another woman, dressed in red, hid behind a tree.

25

A Plan

I spent most of the next day devising a new plan, which I presented to my parents that evening. My proposal was that I would spend the rest of the summer camping along the trail. That way I wouldn't have to trek back and forth each day, and I could speed along with my mission.

'Zinny,' my father said, 'I'm not sure you should be up there alone.'

'Why not?' I said. 'There's nobody around. It's just me and the trees and the birds.'

'What about the lions and tigers?' Sam asked.

'There aren't any lions and tigers, Sam,' Mom said. 'But bobcats, maybe, and deer – and maybe a bear or two—'

I wasn't afraid of deer. I'd heard about the bobcats and bears, but these were just stories, I figured. 'I've never seen anything like that up there,' I said. 'Besides, if I don't bother them, they won't bother me.'

'You're too young,' Dad said.

'Too *young*? Weren't you eleven years old when you drove Uncle Nate's truck from here to Mississippi?'

'Well,' he stumbled, 'times were different then.'

'And Mom, weren't you twelve when you back-packed through Kentucky?'

'Was I only twelve? Times *were* different then . . .'

'It's just hills,' I said. 'Trees and hills and dirt.'

'Zinny,' Dad said, 'I'm not so sure about this trail thing.'

'It's not a trail *thing*—'

Dad scowled. 'You were easier to deal with when you didn't talk, you know that?'

Mom said, 'Don't say that – let her talk.'

'OK,' he said. 'Won't you be crossing other people's property? What if they don't want you carving up their land? You'd be trespassing.'

'It's a public right-of-way,' I said.

'Is it? How do you know that?'

'The lady at the museum told me. It's on all the maps.'

'What maps?'

So I showed them the maps, and even though the lady at the museum hadn't actually told me that it *was* a public right-of-way, once I had said that it was, it sounded reasonable to me, and the more I insisted that it was, the more I believed it.

My parents were impressed by the maps. 'This is amazing,' my father said. 'It goes all the way to Chocton.'

'Zinny,' Mom said, 'I had no idea – why don't you get some help with this project?'

'It isn't a *project*—'

'I don't like the idea of you being up there alone,' Dad said. 'Maybe you could take someone along – one of your brothers, say, or Gretchen?'

From the next room, Gretchen shouted, 'No way!'

'I don't want to take anyone with me. I want to do it alone. It's *my* trail—'

'Zinny, it isn't *your* trail,' Mom said.

'It is, too. And I'm not taking anyone with me.'

'But what if something happened to you? What if you got hurt?'

'I'd come home.'

'But what if you couldn't come home? What if you were knocked unconscious? Or bitten by a snake? Or broke your leg?'

'Good golly,' I said. 'Or what if a plane fell on me? Or a tornado came along and swept me to Canada? Or—'

It went on like that for some time, until Mom said, 'Zinny, you seem awfully anxious to get out of here—'

'Well, I am!' I said. 'It's too crowded here and too noisy. Nothing is mine. Bonnie wears my shoes, Sam took the pillow off my bed, I never have a towel that's my own, nobody knows my name, there's never a clean glass in the cupboard, and somebody swiped my toothbrush.' I didn't think I ought to mention about feeling that if I didn't finish this trail, I was going to be struck down by the hand of God.

Mom and Dad stared at me. Mom said, 'We've never heard you talk like this – you never talked to us—'

'And you never talked to me either!'

They both reared back as if I had thrown a tub of water in their faces, and I should have felt terrible, but my thoughts were jumping around like peas on a hot shovel.

Mom said, 'But you were always at Jessie's – you always talked to *her*—'

I should have let her finish, but I didn't. On I barrelled: 'Up on the trail, everything's mine: the trees, the grass, the air, the flowers. Like Aunt Jessie always said, you need those hyacinths.'

'What's she talking about?' Dad said.

'You know,' Mom said wearily, 'Jessie's hyacinth thingy.' I think that even though she loved Aunt Jessie and missed her, she was getting tired of hearing me refer to Aunt Jessie as the ultimate authority.

'What hyacinth thingy?' Dad asked.

'That wall hanging Jessie embroidered, with the saying about the hyacinths: *Man needs bread and hyacinths: one to feed the body, and one to feed the soul.*'

I saw the wall hanging in my mind. The saying was cross-stitched at the bottom, and at the top were three pictures: a loaf of bread, a bundle of hyacinths, and suspended over the bread and hyacinths was a hand – a large hand. It gave me a shiver to think of it. Aunt Jessie had said it was *the hand of God*.

And instantly I remembered hearing Aunt Jessie say, from time to time, *The Lord giveth, and the Lord taketh away.* Whenever she'd say that, I'd automatically see that hand of God. I'd see it handing out the bread and hyacinths, and then, instantly, snatching them back again. It made me cold to think of it now.

Dad said. 'Whatever happened to that wall hanging?'

'Zinny put it in her coffin, remember?' Mom said.

'Oh yeah.' He tapped his fingers on the table. 'Zinny, this is all about Aunt Jessie isn't it – all this business with the trail?'

'I don't know what you're talking about,' I said.

'We *all* miss her,' he said. 'But you aren't going to find her up there—'

My mother surprised me by saying to him, 'Maybe she will. Maybe Zinny needs to get out of this house for a while.'

We were interrupted by Will, who was carrying four eggs, and by Ben, who was chasing him. 'Give them back!' Ben said.

Will stood beside Mom. 'Look at these! Ben was going to *bury* them – in his squirt garden.'

'Ben?' Mom said. 'Is that true?'

'Yes.'

'Do you mind if I ask *why* you were going to bury them?'

He flushed. 'It's an experiment. I wanted to see what would grow out of them.'

Will went wild. 'Do you believe that? He actually thought he could bury these in the ground and *chickens* would grow out of them.'

'Maybe not a chicken,' Ben said. 'Maybe a chicken bean.'

'What the heck is a chicken bean?' Dad said.

'Do you think we could get back to *me*?' I said. 'The trail. Camping. Me. Remember?'

From the porch came a loud whacking sound,

accompanied by Uncle Nate shouting, 'Dag blast it! Dag blast it!'

We all surged through the door. Uncle Nate was furiously thrashing a coiled piece of rope.

I stood there, watching Uncle Nate beat the rope. I wanted to hug him – or slap him – I wasn't sure which. I wanted to shout, *I miss her too! I miss her most!*

My thoughts were interrupted by Dad. 'OK, Zinny, OK—'

'OK? You mean I can go?'

'No,' Dad said. 'I mean we need a few days to think this over. We're not saying yes, and we're not saying no.'

As Ben sneaked toward his garden, cradling the eggs in his hands, I touched Uncle Nate's shoulder. 'I think it's dead now,' I said.

26

Provisions

Three days later, when I had convinced myself that my parents had forgotten all about my plan and that I'd have to make another plea, they surprised me by telling me that I could go. I nearly fell off the porch from shock. There were, however, conditions:

1. They wanted to see my gear before I set off, and they insisted I include certain safety items: flashlight, flare, matches, knife, and first-aid kit with snake-bite remedy.

2. I had to plan reasonable meals and, although they would pay for the food, I had to go buy it and organize it.

3. I had to promise not to do anything stupid.

4. I had to agree to return home once every ten days (originally they insisted on once a week, but I bargained) so that they could see that I was alive.

5. If a bear ate me, I had to leave a note explaining what had happened. (This last condition was their idea of a joke.)

It took me two days to organize everything. First I made lists of food and equipment, feeling proud of myself for being able to manage with so few items, but my family kept suggesting additions.

'What about water?' Bonnie said. 'Don't you need water?'

'I guess I do,' I admitted, adding water to the list.

'What about fruit and vegetables?' Mom asked. 'You can't just eat canned beans.'

I added fruit and vegetables.

'What about a sleeping bag?' Dad said. 'You can't just sleep on the bare ground. What if it gets cold?'

'And a tent,' Mom said, 'or at least a tarp, for when it rains.'

One sleeping bag and one tarp joined the list.

I rejected the lantern because I already had a flashlight. I also rejected the portable stove because I couldn't lug it up there with everything else I'd already be carrying. Reluctantly, I included a change of clothes because Gretchen made a scene over how disgusting it would be if I wore the same clothes for ten days.

'What do you think the pioneers did?' I had argued. 'Do you think they carted around a suitcase full of clean clothes?'

'I'm sure they did,' Gretchen said.

Mom insisted that I take my toothbrush, and when I reminded her that someone had swiped it, she said, 'You can have mine.'

'No thanks,' I said. 'I'll buy one.'

I felt as if I had that trip planned down to a gnat's eyebrow.

With my food list in hand, I went to Mrs Flint's store. When I saw Jake's truck parked outside, I stewed over whether I should leave and return the next morning, but that would mean another day's wait before I could get up to the trail. I made a firm resolve to be quick, and to keep my mouth shut as much as possible.

'Zinny! Dang it, Zinny! I – you – what – I . . .' He stumbled all over himself, knocking over a pyramid of soup cans he'd been building, and backing into the magazine display. 'Cripes – dang it . . .'

I busied myself gathering the items on my list, crossing them off as I found them. I'd decided not to speak at all.

Jake floundered among the soup cans, attempting to rebuild the display. 'Zinny – cripes – Zinny . . .' He was as nervous as a long-tailed cat in a room full of rocking chairs.

I made a neat pile of the items I'd already selected and returned to the shelves.

'Dang it, Zinny – aren't you even going to say hello?'

'Hello.' That was big of me, I thought.

'Aren't you even going to thank me for the horse?'

'I believe May's the one who should thank you.'

'May? Why May?'

'Because she said you gave it to her.'

'What? I never – to May? It was for you, Zinny.'

'That's not what May says.'

The newly rebuilt pyramid of cans toppled to the floor. 'Cripes . . .'

I crossed off the last item on my list. 'Could you ring these up for me, please?'

He kicked a can across the aisle and stepped to the counter, looking as mad as a trapped hornet. Quickly, he rang up each item, mashing the register keys and roughly shoving each thing aside after he'd entered its price.

In three paper sacks, he dumped the groceries. The bread went on the bottom, cans on top. I wasn't going to argue. It wasn't until I'd paid him that I realized I wasn't going to be able to carry everything. If I couldn't carry it home, how was I going to get it up the trail, along with all my gear?

If it had been Mrs Flint waiting on me, I would have asked her to let me put some things back, but I couldn't ask Jake that, not the way he was scowling at me. Before I could think of what else to do, Jake grabbed two of the bags and headed for the door. He tossed them in the back of his truck, returned for the third bag, and flipped the sign on the door from OPEN to CLOSED. 'Get a move on, Zinny. I don't have all day, you know.'

I climbed in the truck and stared straight ahead. He drove like a madman down the highway, careening around the curves, and spinning into our gravel drive.

'I hate trucks,' I said.

He sped up the hill toward the house, sending gravel flying on all sides. At the first bend, Jake swerved to avoid hitting Uncle Nate as he ran across the drive in front of us. Jake stopped and sat there, white as the moon, while Uncle Nate stared at the truck like a scared deer caught on the highway.

'You've got to stop running around like that,' Jake said. 'You're going to get hurt—'

Uncle Nate blinked and waved his stick. 'The day I can't run, I'd better be dead!'

116

I loved that. I wanted to say, *You tell him, Uncle Nate. You just tell him.*

Jake continued up the drive, more slowly now, shaken by his near miss with Uncle Nate. I felt I had to say something before we got to the house, but I didn't know what to say – words were whirling around in my head like moths fluttering around a light bulb. What I finally said was not what I had intended – it was just what happened to fall out of my mouth: 'What I was looking for was a real horse, not a stupid old wooden horse, and I can get my own horse, thank you very much.'

'Zinny – wait – I have two things to say and you're going to listen. First: I hear you're going to camp up on the trail by yourself. Why don't you let me help you?'

'No. Absolutely not.'

'You are the most stubborn person I ever did meet.'

'What was the other thing you wanted to say?' I didn't want him to be another Tommy Salami. I wanted him to say, *Zinny, I don't care beans about May. It's you I adore.* Or something to that effect.

He gripped the wheel. 'Zinny, I hate to say this, but I need that ring back.'

I froze. 'The ring? Well, Jake, I hate to say *this*, but that ring is gone. Somebody *stole* it.'

I leaped out of the truck, grabbed the bags, and didn't look back. All I heard was squealing tyres and May calling, 'Jake? Jake, wait . . .'

27
Alone

I left early the next morning, and as sure as I live and breathe, that first day on my own lingered on so long I could have sworn there were five hundred hours in it.

Mom and Dad had stumbled out of bed to see me off, poking at my backpack, which was stuffed near to bursting and lashed with rope from which various doodads hung. My sleeping bag and tarp were rolled into a tight sausage and suspended from the bottom of the backpack, and I'd fashioned another pack out of an old flour sack, to carry the food in.

I set up camp where I'd left off the previous day, figuring that each day after working on the trail, I'd walk back to camp, and every two or three days, I would pack it all up and move further ahead. After everything was set up, I sat there, taking in my territory. I'd looked forward to this moment for so long – all by myself up in the hills with the birds and trees and sky, with no one to bother me for ten whole days.

My 'room' wasn't a cramped box shared with three sisters, or invaded by brothers or parents – it was the whole wide-open countryside. I had my food, my water, my tarp, my flashlight, my toothbrush –

all my own, and nobody was going to eat them, stomp on them, or make off with them. In the days before leaving, when I had spun this scene in my mind, I had imagined that I would sit there for hours like that, maybe the whole day, absorbing it all into my skin. But oddly, after about five minutes, I was antsy, and so I grabbed my trowel and started clearing the trail.

I was used to clearing for four or five hours at a stretch, and so this part of the day was normal for me. Whenever I was clearing, it was like when I was scything that time – I wasn't thinking, just moving my arms and hands, which seemed joined to the trowel, the grass, the trail. But sometimes, in the middle of all that non-thinking, or as I was finishing my work, scenes would fly out, suddenly and unexpectedly, from some hidden place in my brain, like little birds rising suddenly from the branches of a tree.

One of these scenes that flew out that day was an image of my parents, sitting there at the table, with my mother saying that I'd always talked to Jessie. In the quiet of the woods I could see my mother's face again, and I saw that hurt look. *She had minded that I'd talked to Jessie.* This came as such a shock. And just before this scene disappeared, I wondered if my mother were replaying that same scene, if she could see me again, and if she heard me saying that she and my father hadn't talked to me. I was hoping she wasn't hearing that, because I was sorry I had said it. And then I started thinking that maybe I had wanted them to talk to me more, to notice me more. But I could hear May again: *Oh, Zinny, how immature!*

I stopped working at four o'clock, the time I'd usually start for home, and it took me a few minutes to realize that I didn't need to go home, that I *was* home. I didn't even need to stop working, if I didn't want to. I could go on for hours – why, I could work all through the night if I wanted.

On my way back to my makeshift campsite, I collected wood for my fire, and decided what I would eat. I'd heat up a can of beans and have a slice of bread and a piece of fruit, topped off with water, and, for dessert, half a chocolate bar. It sounded magnificent. I ran it all through my mind again, how I would build the fire, and open the can of beans. *Open* the can? With a sinking feeling, I knew I'd forgotten to include a can opener.

Why hadn't I thought of such an obvious thing? Why hadn't anyone *reminded* me? Then I remembered all the things they *did* remind me to include, and how they all seemed concerned that I not be cold or hungry, that I be safe. I turned the scene around and saw how muley I'd been, how eager to get away from them. I was feeling like a low-down worm.

I had trouble with the fire. I fumbled and coaxed and pleaded, begging that wood to catch. I tried everything, even yelling at it, but the wood was too damp and too big. Jake probably knew how to build a fire. Maybe I should have let him help me. That thought made me really prickly. I didn't want to think about Jake. I scaled everything down and started with a few dry leaves and two skinny twigs, and once that was going, I added bigger and bigger pieces until it was a roaring bonfire. I overdid it, I admit. Ravenous for those beans, I stabbed and punched one can until it splattered open.

It doesn't take long to eat when you're by yourself. You don't have to wait for anyone to pass things, and you don't have to answer questions. I wished I'd brought a cup, but at least I could swig water out of the bottle. When I finished eating, I wiped off my fork and buried the empty can. There! I didn't have to clear the table or wash the dishes! I was a free and independent person and I could do whatever I liked.

I looked around. What exactly did people do when they had all the time in the world and could do whatever they liked?

From far below came the mournful train whistle, and I instinctively turned in the direction of the farm, thinking of the ash tree and the cardinals and Aunt Jessie and Uncle Nate. My family would be clattering around the dinner table, and I wondered if anyone would notice that I was gone.

Out flew another scene: my parents getting up early that morning to see me off. And another: Sam slurping his soup. And more: Ben in his garden, Gretchen hunched over her computer. *Stop!* I pleaded with my brain. *Stop it!*

It was way too early to sleep. I walked around my campsite, straightening my sleeping bag, stoking the fire, and deciding what I would have for breakfast.

When I realized I would need more wood for the fire, I was thrilled. Something to do! Gather wood!

While I was searching for wood, I remembered the zinnia seeds I had brought. Something else to do! Dragging a stick in each hand, I made a groove along each side of the trail I had cleared that day. As I walked back to my camp, I scattered seeds in the grooves, and then I retraced my steps, tamping the dirt. The seeds should have been watered, but I didn't want to waste my drinking water, so I hoped for rain soon.

These were trivial things my mind focused on, and I knew it, but they kept me from thinking about the bigger things that were lurking behind this clutter. I felt that if I didn't keep busy, a million, million scenes were going to burst out of my head all at once. Part of me was curious to see what was in there, but I wanted to see them slowly, one at a time.

My watch said that it was only seven o'clock, and I shook it, thinking it must have stopped. On another wood search, I found an old maple tree, which would be a great climbing tree, with its sturdy, well-spaced branches. I thought, *hey, I can just climb right up there*. It might seem like a dumb thing to think, but at the time it was a thundering revelation – that I had seen something I wanted to do, and I could go ahead and do it, without worrying that I'd be late or had to finish something else first or that someone might tell me it was dangerous.

So I climbed the tree. Up and up I went, telling myself, *Go on, go higher, you can go as high as you want*. I settled on a branch, high, high above the ground. Birds were chattering, diving and swooping among the trees. Two grey squirrels chased each other up a nearby oak tree, their tails flicking like feathery whips.

Way off and far below was a thin ribbon of the river, and scattered here and there were rooftops and silos and pastures. From my perch, I spotted my trail and my campfire. As I turned to look further up the hill, a dark shape fluttered at the corner of my vision. I turned back to my campsite and again thought I saw a shifting shadow, brief and wavering, like the whisk of a dark cape.

I listened and watched, and although I saw no more movement near my campsite, what I heard made me uneasy. There were creaks and groans that I'd not heard before, snaps and crackles, rattles and drones – a pulsing, thrumming of sound all around me. In a few hours it would be dark, and there I was, alone in a tree high up in the hills, and I was afraid.

I remained there a long time, in a sort of stupor, and might never have moved from that spot, but when the tree itself groaned as if it were tired of supporting my weight, I sat up with a start. My campfire was barely a glow below, and the sun had set, dropping an orange curtain over the sky.

I climbed down, trying to ignore the sounds of the woods and its creatures, and hurried back to my campsite, stoked the fire, and slipped into my sleeping bag. I lay flat on my back staring at the sky, watching the blinking fireflies, and the moths which darted on the fringes of the campfire. Bats swooped overhead. I was waiting for the moment when it would be dark. Then I would close my eyes and sleep.

But there was no moment of dark. Instead, what I saw was the most subtle shading in the sky, a gradual deepening of colour, so gradual that you could not actually see the changes, but could only think, *Is that the colour it was a moment ago? Isn't it deeper now? Is it dark yet? Is this dark?* Soon I noticed the white specks of stars, but still they weren't draped on a black sky, still it wasn't dark. And although I watched intently, I did not see the moment of dark, and I wondered if maybe it wasn't a moment at all.

28

Baby in the Bag

Once in the night I heard a crackling of twigs, as if someone were near. I was burrowed in my sleeping bag, too sleepy and too afraid to look, but I listened. Hearing nothing more, I decided it had been the fire settling, and went back to sleep. I dreamed of baby Rose and the shopping bag.

I must have had lots of memories of Rose, because we were raised like twins, always together. Sometimes we even slept together because we'd put up such a fuss when we were separated. It bothered me that I couldn't resurrect these memories.

One of my teachers once said that we can't get at very early memories because our brains file memories by words, and when we're infants, we don't have enough words. I wasn't sure I believed this, because sometimes I saw baby Rose's face, an infant face, from before either of us knew any words at all.

Maybe it was like Gretchen's computer. Sometimes when she tried to open up a file, the screen flashed *Locked!* or *No access!* Gretchen then pleaded and coaxed, talking to her computer as if it were a naughty child, and if it continued to resist her, she scolded it and flicked it off.

Memories of Rose were locked somewhere, and I

was denied access. That night, however, one snuck out of its locked drawer:

Aunt Jessie emptied a shopping bag and placed it on the floor. It was one of those fancy, sturdy ones, wide and tall, made of heavy-duty paper with two handles. Rose crawled into it, and Aunt Jessie picked it up, saying, 'Oh, I guess I'll go shopping, la-de-da', and swinging the bag back and forth. 'Has anyone seen my Rose?' she said. 'La-de-da.'

I peeked into the bag and there was Rose all curled up, grinning away, and I looked up at Aunt Jessie, and she, too, was smiling and laughing, and it was the most wonderful thing to see. Aunt Jessie asked me if I wanted a turn in the bag, but I didn't. I wanted to see Rose in it, grinning, and Aunt Jessie swinging that bag saying, 'La-de-da.'

My dream was exactly how it had been, except that in the dream, the scene played over and over, and I stood to one side, praying that it would never, ever end.

In the morning a thin band of copper seeped above the horizon, and dew clung to cobweb bridges woven through the grass. In this peaceful scene, I wondered how I could have been so afraid the night before.

That day, I fell into a routine that I followed for the next eight days. I'd head out early, admiring my recently cleared stretch of trail, which I was clearing more rapidly – at least a half-mile a day, and sometimes twice that much.

Each day, I'd find something to add to my growing collection of things found along the trail: arrowheads, flints, strips of leather, bits of rope, a bowie knife, and a slingshot. I knew that the lady at the historical museum would blow a gasket if she could see these things. I also found fossils. In low-lying areas, there were plant fossils and brachiopods that looked like clams. Aunt Jessie would have had a grin a mile wide, and she would've said these were sure-fire proof that the area had been a huge sea millions and millions of years ago.

Depending on what I'd find, I'd be, for the rest of the day, a trapper cat-stepping through the forest, or an archaeologist on a major dig, or an escaped convict fleeing his jailers. Often I returned to being *Zinny Taylor: detective*, searching for Jake's ring and the medallion. The more I thought about them, the more I believed they were connected to the trail, and if I kept going, I would find more clues.

I wondered about Uncle Nate's treks through the hills, and if he might have taken the medallion and the ring, but I couldn't imagine why he'd want them or what he would do with them.

Shortly after noon on that second day, the quiet was disturbed by the buzz of a small plane. A single-engine crop duster zipped over the trees, and I thought I was about to be sprayed with insecticide, though I couldn't imagine why anyone would be spraying up there. The plane circled overhead, and the two men seated up front waved. As I waved back, the plane dipped and turned, and I saw that the passenger was my father. 'You don't have to check on me!' I shouted. He couldn't hear me, but he smiled and waved again. Every couple days after that, he'd buzz by, hitching a ride with the crop duster, and it got so I missed him on the days he didn't come.

In the evenings after dinner at the camp, I'd gather wood and plant zinnia seeds along the new stretch, and usually I'd climb a tree and wait for the six o'clock train whistle. The next few hours – between the whistle and dark – were the hardest, and for the first several days at this time, I had to force myself not to flee down the trail for home.

On the fourth day, I moved my camp ahead. During the early evening hours, I began to notice things in the woods, little things, normal things, like grasshoppers, crickets, butterflies, and moths zinging through the grass. Bordering the sentries of oaks, elms, beeches, and larches grew scores of wildflowers: buttercups and goldenrod; daisies and black-eyed susans; goat's-beard and lady's-slippers. In my head I could hear Aunt Jessie saying, 'Bingo!' and 'What a wonder!' She and Uncle Nate had taught me to recognize all these things.

Sometimes, one grasshopper or one fossil or one maple would be mesmerizing. You could look at any one of these for days and weeks and months, and you'd see something different each time. Maybe it was the same with people: if you studied them, you'd see new and different things. But would you like what you saw? Did it depend on who was doing the looking?

I marked my progress on the trail maps. Already I'd passed through all of Maiden's Walk, which straddled the fenced meadow (though the meadow wasn't on the original map), and dipped through Crow

Hollow, a shallow valley ringed with tall maples and inhabited by hundreds of jabbering crows.

I'd cleared straight across Baby Toe Ridge – weak-kneed and cringing, because on the back of the map was a handwritten legend which made me uneasy. A baby had been kidnapped by a wolf, and the only remains of the baby ever found were three toes, discovered on this ridge. As if that wasn't gruesome enough, this note was added: *Several sightings of baby's ghost on ridge.*

Twice, after working on this stretch of trail, I dreamed about baby Rose. In one of these dreams, someone was peering at her in the dresser drawer and saying, *Where are her toes?*

The old logging railroad was now rusted tracks ending abruptly in the middle of the woods. On either side of the railroad yawned clearings where trees had been felled. Old stumps still bearing the marks of cross-cut saws squatted here and there. There were also apple trees, which seemed out of place. I wondered if maybe loggers had brought apples up the hill with them, and tossed their cores aside, and after the men were long gone, after the railroad was shut down, apple saplings snuck out of their dark caves.

I was always in a muddle about time. It didn't seem like a series of days, but one stretch of time, with light and dark blending into each other. Time went on and on; it didn't start and stop, as I had thought. If time didn't start and stop, I thought, maybe life didn't either. Maybe it just went on and on and on.

And I'd dream about Rose going on and on and Aunt Jessie going on and on, and I'd dream about my family, and Jake, and everyone was going on and on, and I'd wake up and I'd look around and I'd be surprised that there wasn't a whole gang of people sitting there staring at me.

29

Glimpses

On a maple stick, I carved a notch each morning, fearing that if I didn't, I'd lose all sense of time, and might forget to go home on the tenth day as I had promised. Whenever I heard the train whistle, I still had terrible longings and would think about running down the trail and seeing the farm below and dashing into the kitchen and there everyone would be.

There was another source of unease, more difficult to explain. Several times I glimpsed a fluttering at the corner of my sight, or a moving shadow, or a spot of colour – often red – as of someone's sleeve or cap, ducking behind a tree. I'd halt, wait, listen, suspecting that someone was near, watching me, spying on me. Sometimes I thought it was Aunt Jessie I was seeing, and that she was there in the woods, watching over me. Once, I confess, I chased after that flicker of red, hoping it was her red hair I'd seen, but when I found nothing, I worried that I was becoming like Uncle Nate, chasing air. Pretty soon I'd be carrying a stick and beating lifeless things to death with it.

I felt guilty when I thought about Uncle Nate. I kept thinking that if I'd never been born, Rose wouldn't have caught whooping cough and Aunt

Jessie wouldn't have been scared by a snake and crawled into a drawer, and Uncle Nate wouldn't ever be alone, chasing after his Redbird day and night, and he wouldn't need another sweetheart. I wanted to put Time on a big reel and wind it back so that the three of them could be together again. Whenever I imagined this, I'd think maybe I could just snip me out of it, but I'd keep seeing myself there with Rose and Uncle Nate and Aunt Jessie, and I didn't want to snip myself out of it. I wanted to be there, and I wanted to be here now, and I didn't want to be erased.

Then I'd think, *Well, what am I doing up here in the woods?* Had I erased myself from my family, down there in the farm far below? I didn't have a good answer for that, but I had the eerie feeling that I wasn't erasing Zinny; I was looking for her – as if I was invisible, but Zinny was out there somewhere. Other times, I thought I was looking for Rose, looking for Aunt Jessie, and they'd be there on the trail, waiting for me.

Once, as I crawled into my sleeping bag, I saw a flicker of reddish orange, and I sat still, wanting to chase it, but forcing myself not to. Stealthily, a fox moved into the clearing and stared at me, poised and alert on slender black legs. Bushy rust-coloured fur surrounded a puff of white at its throat, and pointed ears stood erect, listening intently. It studied me, narrowing its eyes as if it knew me, and then it vanished.

I was left sitting there thinking about ants, who would be eaten by grasshoppers, and grasshoppers who would be eaten by birds, who might, in turn,

be eaten by foxes, who might then be eaten by . . .
Nothing was safe; everything was in danger of being
gobbled up by something else. Even me – I could
be gobbled up too, like baby Rose and Aunt Jessie.

One night I dreamed that I was running through
a maze with high green hedges, chasing a bumblebee
as big as a bird. Behind me, panting, lurched a huge
tiger carrying a stick in his brilliant white teeth.

It was the morning after this dream that I found
the cup amid the cans of beans. I hadn't brought a
cup, or so I thought, but there it was. The next day,
a can opener. Two days later I found the soap. I
hadn't brought soap, had I? I was a bit worried about
my brain.

On the ninth day, I reached Sleepy Bear Ridge.
This portion of the trail had been well carved: a
solid, flat plateau about two feet wide, etched into
the side of the hill. A rocky, grassy stretch rose to the
left, and there, resting on the top of the ridge, was a
black rock which resembled a bear curled on its side.
Below the trail, the hill was banked with tall larch
trees, in small groups, with clearings in between.
There were no stones on the trail, and there had
probably never been stones here. The natural
drainage of the land made this a dry, secure path.
All I needed to do here was to clear some of the
more overgrown sections.

From the top of the bear-shaped rock, I had a
terrific view down over the mountainside and larch
groves, and it was from this point that I spotted the
roof of a small cabin below the trail. It was the first

dwelling of any kind I'd seen so near the trail, and I suspected it was abandoned.

At the far end of this curved portion of the trail, about a mile away, the path slid into deep, dark trees, eerie and forbidding. On the map, this new area was marked as Spook Hollow. Spook Hollow would have to wait, for I was going home the next day.

30

Homecoming

I had planned to clear part of the trail before heading home on the tenth day, but when I awoke just before sunrise, it was raining. This was all the excuse I needed to leave straight away, and once I'd made that decision, I was surprised at how eager I was to go home.

I secured my things beneath the tarp, taking with me only my backpack and food sack, and set off down the trail. In some ways it seemed that time had raced by – already it was the tenth day, already I was heading home – but in other ways it seemed that I'd been gone for months. I kept trying to remember what everyone looked like, and to guess how they'd react when they saw me. How happy they'd be to see me again, safe and sound, not shrivelled from hunger or mauled by a bear.

When I had agreed to come home every ten days, I imagined that I would dash in, grace them with my presence for a few minutes, shovel more food in my pack, and race back to my camp. Now, as I walked proudly down my trail, crossing the old railroad, I thought I might spend the whole day at home, maybe even the night. I'd do it as a favour to my family, I told myself, so that they wouldn't feel too entirely miserable at my dashing in and out as if I couldn't stand to be there. But really it would be a favour to me: I wanted to be there.

No sooner had I decided to stay the night than I had doubts. They would think I was homesick. Maybe they were happier with me gone, anyway; maybe they would be annoyed if I came back and got in everyone's way.

As I started across Baby Toe Ridge, I saw someone ahead of me on the trail. It was Jake Boone with a backpack slung over his shoulder. When he turned off the trail to head down the hillside, I called to him. He practically jumped out of his skin.

'Zinny? What the heck . . .?'

I nearly dissolved into a puddle at the sound of a human voice. 'What exactly are you doing up here, Jake?'

'Cripes . . .'

'Have you been spying on me?'

'Cripes . . .'

'You were, weren't you? You brought the cup and the soap and the can opener, didn't you?' Everything was coming out all wrong. I didn't want to sound like this.

'Cripes . . .'

'Can't you say anything besides "Cripes"? What do you think you're doing, spying on me like that?'

'Cri— Zinny, I don't exactly call it spying. I was watching over you—'

'I don't need any watching over.' Why were these words coming out of my mouth? Part of me was happy that he'd wanted to protect me, and that he'd brought me things I'd forgotten, but another part of me was all blown up like a toad. I'd wanted to do this by myself. I needed to. I didn't know why, either, and that made me even madder. I zapped him again: 'And where were you sneaking off to just now?'

'Cripes. Down there. It's a shortcut to an old dirt road where I left the truck.'

'Well, go on then. Who's stopping you?'

'Come on, I'll give you a lift.'

'No thanks. I'm going down the trail. *My* trail.'

'You're as hard as a stone, Zinny Taylor.' Then he nearly knocked me off my feet by yanking me toward him. He seemed so tall all of a sudden. I could smell pine on his shirt, and little beads of sweat were trickling down his neck.

My mouth stopped yapping. I was going to stand there for ever and I would never speak again and time would go on and on and on. Jake put one soft hand on each side of my face and leaned down and placed a kiss on my mouth. Right there on my *lips*. I nearly vaporized into the atmosphere. Before I could blink, though, he stepped back and said, 'Might as well give you something to really get in a duck fit about!' And as I stood there like a stone, he sauntered off down the hill.

When I regained my senses, I was so flustered I didn't know what to do. 'You *worm*!' I called. 'You – you – *complete worm*!' Really. Sometimes I am such a jerk. He wasn't a worm at all. I hoped he hadn't heard me.

I took off across Baby Toe Ridge and ran down the trail, through Crow Hollow, and on through the first part of Maiden's Walk. But I stopped short when I came to the fenced meadow, where I had cut the barbed wire and laid the stones. 'Cripes!' I said. Someone had repaired the barbed wire and hung a sign on it: NO TRESPASSING!

The stones still lay across the meadow, and there was no sign of anyone or of any animals. My wire cutters were miles back at the camp. It was easy enough to get through the fence by stretching the wires apart, but I'd have to make a more permanent arrangement. I'd have to cut them again. No trespassing? The owners obviously didn't know about the public right-of-way. I could no longer remember whether it was true about the trail being a public right-of-way, or whether I'd made that up, but that seemed of little importance.

Farther down the trail, I checked the place where I'd found the medallion and where I'd later buried the ring. The hole was still empty.

On down the trail I went until there it was: the farm, as if newly planted for my eyes only. That big wonderful barn, with its funny lopsided doors. That green grass, those stately trees. That sweet, sweet house sitting by itself in the clearing, with the tall oak leaning toward my bedroom window. It was a beautiful landscape, a magnificent miniature world.

It was early yet, and so I stopped at the creek to look for Poke. I dug up a few worms, and, as if in answer to my offering, Poke emerged from beneath an overhanging rock, lifting his head toward me tentatively. I laid the worms on a leaf and waited. Inch by inch, Poke crept up the bank, and behind him followed another, smaller turtle.

I went on up to the house, wondering why I was suddenly so nervous, why I felt like a stranger trespassing. The house was unusually quiet. Were they expecting me? Were they planning a surprise?

I crossed the porch and entered the kitchen. No one in sight, no sounds of anyone. The door to Uncle Nate's was closed. Upstairs, my parents' bedroom was empty. The boys' door was open, and inside, the three of them were curled up, sound asleep. Were they pretending? I touched Ben's foot, which was sticking out beneath his blanket. He murmured and kicked, as if shaking off a fly. In my room, not only were my sisters asleep, but someone was in my bed. A tousled head of brown hair rested on my pillow.

It was not exactly the homecoming I had hoped for.

31

Dag-blasted Body

When I sat on the edge of Bonnie's bed, she opened her eyes, blinked sleepily, and said, 'Oh, hi.'

'Where are Mom and Dad?' I asked.

'Mm? Aren't they here? Maybe Dad's at work. He had an emergency or something, I think. Mom's probably watching Uncle Nate.'

'Why?'

She yawned. 'I'm not hardly half awake, Zinny. Don't you know about Uncle Nate?'

'Know what?'

'He hurt himself – guess how.'

I felt cold, afraid. 'How?'

'Doing the boogie-woogie.'

'Is he here? Is he OK?'

'Of course he's here, Zinny. He told Dad he'd shoot himself before he'd go to a hospital.'

'I've got to see him,' I said. 'By the way, who's in my bed?'

'Shh. You'll wake her. That's Junie.'

I hadn't the vaguest idea who Junie was, but she sure looked comfortable. I had another one of those odd feelings – maybe that was Zinny in the bed, and I was someone else. It gave me the creeps.

Downstairs, I went through to Uncle Nate's and

inched open his bedroom door. Mom was dozing in a chair near his bed, and Uncle Nate lay flat on his back, wide awake, clutching his stick. I didn't like to see him like that, confined to his bed.

'Shh,' he said, but Mom had already heard me.

'Zinny!' she said, leaping up to hug me. 'I knew you'd be fine. I knew you'd be back when you said. You'll have to tell us everything. Here, sit down. Will you stay with Nate while I get some breakfast ready?'

I stood there like an old dead tree trunk. She looked so different. Had her hair always curled like that at the temples? Had she always had those creases by her eyes?

She turned at the door to glance back at me. 'I knew you'd be fine,' she repeated. 'I knew it.'

I sat beside Uncle Nate. 'Want to get up?' I asked.

'Cain't.'

'What do you mean?'

'Cain't do it.'

'You hurt your leg?'

'Dag-blasted leg. Dag-blasted heart. Dag-blasted body.'

'What's wrong with your heart?'

'It jumps.'

Mom poked her head through the doorway. 'Don't get him too excited, Zinny. Don't upset him. Just stay there a minute. I'll be back in a jiffy.'

'Pumpkin,' Uncle Nate whispered, beckoning me closer.

'What is it?'

'I oughta be dead.'

'Don't say that! You'll be OK. You'll get better.'

'I cain't run.' He pressed his hands against his face.

Something inside me was splintering into a zillion little pieces.

After Mom came back, I went out to the front porch and sat in the swing, staring at the ash tree for a long, long time. Why did people get old? Why did people get sick? Why couldn't the hand of God fix whooping cough? Why couldn't it snatch a woman back from a drawer? Why couldn't it fix Uncle Nate? I couldn't stand it. I wanted answers to my questions, and I wanted them *immediately*.

It was a strange day. At first I felt as if I were an alien who had just landed in paradise. The most ordinary things startled me. Running water – what a miracle! Toilets! Milk! Eggs! Toast! Television! Electricity! Hearing voices was a delicious treat, and when someone laughed, I thought: *What a perfect sound that is*.

Sam rushed out of the room, returning a few minutes later with Ben. 'See?' Sam said. 'I told you she was crying.'

'Zinny?' Ben said. He put his face up close to mine. 'You're crying.'

I loved that face. I loved every single thing about his perfect face.

Although my family didn't make a huge fuss over me as I had hoped, they did make a little fuss as, one by one, they noticed that I'd returned. Eventually they each got around to asking, 'How is it up there, camping and all?'

I was full up to the top of my head with things to

say, but then Will asked for the milk, and Gretchen said, 'At least you don't have to do any chores,' and then Sam jumped in, and whatever I'd been thinking was lost in the clattering of dishes or wailing complaints ('Ben's taken my shirt – make him give it back!').

My mother and Ben seemed most intrigued. 'It's amazing what you're doing, Zinny,' my mother said. 'Simply amazing. You should hear your dad talk about how far you've gotten. He loves tracking your progress from the air.'

'Gosh,' Bonnie said. 'I could never stay outside all night.' She shuddered. 'Too creepy.'

'And look at you,' Mom said. 'You look so fit and healthy. Good for you, Zinny. Good for you.'

Good for you. This had a strange effect on me. Had I actually done something good? Or had something good happened to me? That phrase kept rolling around in my brain: *Good for you*.

'Have you seen any snakes yet?' Ben asked, and then seemed disappointed when I said I hadn't.

'Want to come up there with me, Ben?' Was this *me* talking? Was I actually inviting someone to join me?

He thought a minute. 'Maybe another time.'

'Afraid of the snakes?' Bonnie said.

'No, I am not,' Ben said. 'I've got to watch my garden.'

I wanted to tell them everything – about light and darkness and time and the creatures and the fox with the staring eyes and the shadows and hearing the train whistle and thinking of home. I wanted to tell them about Maiden's Walk and Baby Toe Ridge and Crow Hollow, but I didn't know how to explain. Besides, they weren't used to hearing me jabber on, and after a few hours, I lapsed into my old silent Zinny self.

The second half of the day, I became fidgety and irritable. Inside the house, I felt like a caged animal, and I'd escape to the porch or the yard, where I'd inhale gulps of air. The sound of human voices became overwhelming – all that chattering, all those loud whoops and shouts. Noises assaulted me: chairs scraping on the floor, the computer bleeping, dishes clattering, footsteps thumping overhead, doors slamming, phones ringing, music blaring.

Once, when Ben, Sam, and Bonnie were all yapping at once, and May was screaming upstairs about a missing hairbrush, I fled to the squirt gardens. Ben's row was immaculate: completely weedless, with perfectly upright bean plants staked like a row of thin soldiers at attention, their pale beans hanging like limp fingers.

I'd been wary of seeing my squirt garden, feeling guilty that I'd neglected it all summer. I expected to see a tangled mass of weeds choking the tomatoes and zinnias. *Wrong!* The tomatoes were firm and green, well staked, free of weeds and bugs, and surrounded by healthy zinnias in full bloom.

Someone had been caring for my garden, and that should have touched me, but in my moody state, it annoyed me. Someone had *interfered*, someone had *taken over* my garden, just as someone had taken over my bed.

Grumpily, I stomped back to the house, and rammed things into my backpack: a change of clothes, toothpaste, and zinnia seeds. I made out a new food list, burrowed into my closet where my money was hidden, and headed for Mrs Flint's store.

32

A Beaut

As I left the drive and turned onto the main road, a
shiny red convertible pulled up beside me. 'Hey,
Zinny!' *Oh that voice!* It was Jake, tanned and
scrubbed, in a white T-shirt and blue jeans, his hair
mussed. I couldn't look at him. I didn't dare. I kept
walking, as his car crept along beside me. 'Zinny –
wait. Where you going?'

'Mrs Flint's.'

'The store? Come on, I'll give you a lift.' He
stopped, jumped out, and opened the passenger door.
'Come on, it's hotter than blazes. It'll save your feet.'

My feet didn't need saving, but I climbed in the
car. This was going to be it, I thought. I was going
to know – there would be another sign – whether
Jake really liked me or not. My heart was saying, *Of
course he does – the kiss, the kiss*, but, strangely, my
head was saying this, *The Lord giveth, and the Lord
taketh away*. It was as if I thought that a hand was
going to drop down from the heavens and snatch
Jake from the driver's seat.

'It's a beaut – don't you think?' he asked, running
his hand across the dashboard.

I was gripping the door handle, keeping my eyes

on the road, forcing my voice to be steady. 'Where'd you get it?'

'It's a beaut,' he repeated, ignoring my question. 'I know you don't like trucks, but how about this? Isn't it a beaut?'

Try to sound normal, Zinny. Try to sound like your normal muley self. 'Yeah, it's a beaut. Where'd you get it?'

'You're really making progress on that trail.'

'You oughta know, I guess. Where'd you get this car?'

He pulled up about fifty yards from Mrs Flint's store. 'Look,' he said, 'I don't want to see Mrs Flint right now, so I'll wait for you here, OK?'

I waited a minute, expecting another kiss or some passionate announcement, but he kept scanning the road and wouldn't look at me. I got out and slammed the door. So much for passion.

He was right about one thing, though – that car was a *beaut*.

'Golly,' Mrs Flint said, when I'd stacked my provisions on the counter. 'You're the one clearing some trail or something, aren't you? You're . . .'

'Zinny.'

'That's right. Zinny.' The phone rang. Mrs Flint sounded agitated. 'I sure don't know,' she complained to the caller, 'and I'm about to give up on that boy. Late again and refusing to work nights and straggling in like a zombie. I told his mother a thing or two when she came in here yesterday. She doesn't know what to do with him either. He doesn't come home most nights, and won't tell her where he's been, and she thinks he's up to no good—' Mrs Flint stopped herself. 'I'll call you back. I've got a customer.'

So. Jake really had been up on the trail watching over me most nights. He wouldn't go to all that trouble if it was May he cared about.

The sheriff walked in. 'Hey there,' he said to Mrs Flint. 'Hey there – which one are—'

'Zinny.'

'Zinny? You the one doing that trail thing? Heard your dad talking about it. Better be careful up there.'

'I will.'

'I'll take one of those candy bars,' he said to Mrs Flint. 'And a red pop.'

'Where you headed?' Mrs Flint asked him.

'On up to the Fosters. They're all in a flutter.'

'Not that cow again?'

'Naw – something about a stolen car. I couldn't make much sense of it. Betty was half hysterical. You know how she gets.'

I struggled out the door with my sacks of groceries, and wasn't real surprised to see that Jake and his beaut of a car were gone. Automatically, I scanned the sky, as if I were looking for traces of a big old hand disappearing back into the clouds.

33

The Old Lady

Straggling home, loaded down with groceries and worries, a glimpse of my shadow frightened me. Was that me – that bent figure creeping along? *Zip!* Out of the no-access portion of my brain slipped another memory of Rose.

After Mom's great-aunt had visited us once, Rose started doing a peculiar thing. She would hunch over and hobble along, her face all scrunched up into a little prune.

'Rose is being an old lady,' Aunt Jessie said.

I started doing it with Rose. People would say, 'Rose and Zinny – do the old lady,' and we'd instantly transform ourselves into miniature old women, creeping through the house grimacing. Aunt Jessie would clap her hands and toss her head back, tickled to pieces.

Not long after baby Rose died, I leaped off a chair one morning and started doing the old lady. I was hoping to cheer up Aunt Jessie, sitting so forlornly on her sofa. She didn't laugh, though. Instead, she said, 'Rose will never be an old lady.'

I never did the old lady again.

*

As I walked on up the road with the sacks of groceries, I thought about what Aunt Jessie had said. Rose never would be an old lady. She would always be four years old and cute and completely innocent, and I envied her.

34

Even a Monkey . . .

Twice I dropped the groceries on my way home, and when one sack split, I had to cram its contents into the two remaining bags. As I turned into our drive, Jake sped past in the red car. Twenty feet beyond me, he honked, braked suddenly, but shot forward again. A minute later, the sheriff's car whizzed past in the same direction, red lights flashing.

Jake had really done it this time. I hoped he wouldn't be arrested. If he were, maybe he would blame me. He might tell the sheriff he'd been trying to impress me, and I'd been such a pill.

Jake's stealing was worrying me. I was all mixed up about it. If anyone else had stolen anything, I would've instantly known it was wrong, wrong, wrong. But with Jake, I'd find myself making excuses for him. Maybe he thought Bingo was mistreated at the Butlers'; maybe he was trying to save Bingo. Maybe he'd borrowed his mother's ring. Maybe he'd borrowed the car.

These excuses didn't convince me. Maybe he couldn't help himself. Maybe he was just a generous, free-hearted sort of person who wanted to make people happy. Maybe he loved me so much that he had lost his senses.

And then I was really mixed up. I was impressed that someone would go to all these lengths just for me. And then I felt guilty that I might be the cause of Jake doing terrible things. And then I worried that something terrible was going to happen to Jake, and then I'd *really* feel guilty. Then I wondered why I was thinking about Jake so much, and did I really like him, and if so, *why* did I like him? And then I got angry that he was making me so confused.

At home, Mom said, 'Are you packing up again already?'

'Yup.'

'We've missed you, Zinny—'

From overhead came a loud crash, followed by Sam's wail, 'Mom . . .' She dashed upstairs.

'You're not spending the night, are you?' Bonnie asked.

'Nope.'

'I want you to stay, Zinny – it's just that Junie's staying, and I was hoping she could have your bed—'

'Fine.'

When Mom returned, she said, 'You've got to stay until your father gets home, and I was hoping you'd stay and help with Uncle Nate tonight . . .'

'Tonight?'

'Your father and I have been taking turns sitting up with him all night, and we're so tired we can hardly stand up. Maybe you could sit with him tonight?'

'What about May or Gretchen or—?'

'They'd be no good at it. They'd fall asleep and

152

wouldn't hear an elephant crash through the window.'

'What about Bonnie?'

'Bonnie's got Junie staying over.'

'The boys?'

'They're too little. Will you do it?'

I didn't want to watch Uncle Nate. I didn't want to see him like that. But I agreed. 'OK, but I'm leaving first thing in the morning,' I said.

In Uncle Nate's room, I curled up in the chair. He was asleep, still clutching that stick. On the wall next to the bed was a framed wall hanging that Aunt Jessie had cross-stitched. At the top, in blue letters, were these words: *Even a monkey falls from a tree.* In the picture below this saying, a monkey tumbled out of a palm tree. I'd always wondered about that monkey, who looked surprised, suspended in the air, forever falling. I wished he could be back in his tree, safe. I didn't want him to crunch to the ground.

Tucked into the mirror frame above the dresser was the 'proof' picture. On top of the dresser was Uncle Nate's camera. Where were Aunt Jessie's lotions and perfume? Her hand mirror?

Her things were vanishing, just like baby Rose's had. There were no reminders of baby Rose anywhere. This had always seemed so sad to me, this erasure of baby Rose from their lives.

Swish! Out flew an image of a pair of dolls that Aunt Jessie had made for me and baby Rose when we were three years old. They were life-sized dolls (three-year-old sized), soft and floppy, dressed in our own clothes. Baby Rose's doll had soft yellow hair, and mine had dark hair. What had happened to those dolls? I longed to see them.

I was gripped by the need to look in that bottom dresser drawer, and tiptoed across the room to open it.

Their marriage quilt was folded neatly, taking up most of the drawer. I patted it tentatively, as if reassuring myself that there was no dead body wrapped in it. To one side, and partially covered by the quilt, was a square black box. Startled by a snore from Uncle Nate, I closed the drawer.

In the pink bathroom, I looked everywhere for the key to the locked cabinet drawer. I ran my hands along the top of the window frame, searched the remaining cabinet drawers, and opened every bottle and jar on the counter. No key.

I returned to Uncle Nate's room and stared out the window. Maybe Uncle Nate and Aunt Jessie had replaced Rose with me. Was it possible that Uncle Nate would ever replace Aunt Jessie with someone else?

Then I heard the cricket. Automatically, I counted his chirps, watching the second hand on Uncle Nate's clock. Seventy-seven degrees outside.

Uncle Nate awoke with a start and said, 'Rose?'

'No, it's Zinny.'

He looked at me for a long, long time. 'I knew it,' he said.

'Uncle Nate, you don't happen to know anything about a medallion, do you?'

'A what?'

As I described it for him, he fidgeted with the sheets. 'Don't talk to me about it,' he said. 'Stop talking.'

'Why? Do you know where it is?'

'Don't talk to me about it.'

I studied him. He looked guilty and afraid. 'Did you take it?'

'I never. Stop it. My heart's jumping.'

I was in my *Zinnia Taylor: detective* mode, and there was no stopping me. I was heartless.

'Where were you really going on those mountain walks? Were you meeting someone?'

He grabbed his stick and raised it in the air. 'Stop it! Stop it!'

I was so angry it scared me. I left the room and paced the hall. Up and down, up and down. I didn't want to hate Uncle Nate. I loved him as much as I loved my own father. More. I loved him more.

What a thought! It went through me like a hundred little lightning bolts. I knew Uncle Nate better than I knew my own father, and I'd known Aunt Jessie better than my own mother.

When I looked back in the room, Uncle Nate appeared to be asleep. I opened the bottom dresser drawer again, and removed the black box. Inside was – *aha!* – the medallion – and a key.

The key fitted the bathroom drawer. I'm not sure what I was expecting, but I was surprised by what I found. There was a box, nearly full, of syringes, and an insulin pamphlet. In all the time I'd known Aunt Jessie and heard her talk about her 'sugar', I'd never known she'd taken insulin shots.

But there was more in the drawer, beneath these things. In a pink heart-shaped box was a locket containing a wisp of hair. Folded beneath the box was a child's drawing of a stick-figure woman and M-O-M in crooked letters.

I touched the hair, and ran my fingers over the drawing. It was Rose's hair and Rose's drawing. What bothered me was that these two things seemed to be all that Aunt Jessie had saved to remind her of Rose, and that she had locked them away in a bath-room drawer.

Uncle Nate was mumbling in his sleep. Once he said, 'Bury it,' and another time he said, 'Redbird!' and, worst of all, he kept saying, 'Let me out of here! Let me out!'

I couldn't bear it. His legs jerked under the sheet and sweat rolled down his forehead. With a cool cloth I mopped his face, and when I tried to straighten his pillow, I found a silken cloth tucked beneath it: Aunt Jessie's embroidery about the hya-cinths, the one I had placed in her coffin with her. There were the hyacinths, the bread, and that hand coming down from the sky.

This really spooked me. How did this get out of the coffin and under Uncle Nate's pillow?

'Redbird! Redbird!' he called.

I held his pillow and looked down on his contorted face, and I don't know what came over me. I was somebody else. I was God. I placed the pillow over his face, blotting it out. I pressed hard.

35

Leaving

As I hurried up the trail early the next morning, I couldn't bear to look back at the house and the farm. If I stole one look, it might suck me up and imprison me.

I kept returning to that moment when I pressed the pillow down on Uncle Nate's face. I was full of love and full of hate. I hated his being sick, trapped like that. I hated myself for thinking that he might replace Aunt Jessie with someone else. And mixed in with this hate was huge, overpowering love for Uncle Nate, my Uncle Nate who wouldn't hurt a flea, who so desperately missed Aunt Jessie, who so desperately wanted to be with her.

When I pressed on the pillow, I was thinking, *Catch her, then, catch her!*

His hand flapped in the air, caught my wrist, and squeezed it. I saw my hands. They were my hands, not God's hands. I snatched the pillow away from Uncle Nate's face.

He stared up at me, and that stare was like the beady eyes of the salamander and the knowing eyes of the fox. I fluffed the pillow and placed it beneath his head. Then I folded Aunt Jessie's hyacinth embroidery and slid it under the pillow. All the while he watched me. I sat in the chair beside his bed and squeezed his hand all night long. Neither of us said a word.

When I heard Mom groping in the kitchen, I snatched Uncle Nate's camera, stuffed it in my backpack, and gathered my food.

'You're up early,' Mom said. 'Leaving already?'

'Yup.'

'How did Uncle Nate sleep?'

'Fine,' I lied.

'Zinny, I want to ask you something.'

I winced, afraid that she knew what I'd done.

'Can you come home next Saturday – instead of in ten days?'

'Why?'

'We're all going to the circus in Chocton.'

'I don't want to go,' I said.

'Are you sure? We're all going.'

'Uncle Nate?' I asked.

'Oh. Right. Well. If you don't want to go to the circus, maybe you'd come home and stay with him? Would you, Zinny? How about it? What's the matter?'

'Nothing.'

'Are you upset about Uncle Nate?' she asked.

I couldn't answer. I yearned to tell her everything – but everything was jumbled up in one big spaghetti pot. Uncle Nate and Jake and Rose and Jessie and the ring and the medallion and the trail were all twisted around in a huge tangle of guilt, and I longed to empty that whole pot into someone else's lap. I wanted to stop feeling guilty about baby Rose and

Aunt Jessie and Uncle Nate. I wanted to understand what Jake was doing and why, and I wanted to stop feeling guilty for his stealing.

Instead, I felt like the monkey in Aunt Jessie's wall hanging: frozen, forever falling, falling, falling.

I ached to be like Sam, stirring his soup saying, 'Don't blame me,' and to be like baby Rose, perpetually *doing* the old lady without actually *being* one, and eternally riding around in a shopping bag pleasing Aunt Jessie.

All of that I wanted to tell my mother, but instead, a faint voice came out of my mouth, and I agreed to come back and watch Uncle Nate the next Saturday.

'Bless you, Zinny.' She helped me strap on my backpack and added, 'Have you said good-bye to him?'

No! I nearly screamed. *I can't! I won't!* But my legs moved toward his room and my hand opened his door and when I leaned down to say good-bye, he whispered, 'Take me up on the trail, Zinny. Take me.'

'I can't . . . you can't—'

'Please, pumpkin,' he begged.

'I can't. Look at you . . .'

He pressed my fingers to his lips. *Tootle-ee-ah-dah . . .*

I couldn't answer. I fled.

It was drizzling as I climbed the trail, and a silvery sheen covered the stones. The mist felt cool against my face, and as I walked along, I scattered zinnia seeds recklessly, bent over like that little old lady, and obsessed with finishing my trail.

Without realizing it, I'd veered off the trail to the spot where the medallion had been buried, and was filled with unaccountable dread. There was a flicker, like a dream re-forming, of me hurrying, running through the woods, running away, kneeling at this spot.

I turned back to the trail and stomped along. As I entered dark Maiden's Walk, I thought, *Here I go, being dragged toward a dark pit, helpless and chained.* But I wasn't going to scream or resist. *Take me,* I begged. *Do away with me.*

The clear light of the meadow was my temporary reprieve. When I came to the barbed-wire fence with its new NO TRESPASSING sign, the meadow was occupied. A sleek chestnut mare paced at the far edge of the fenced enclosure. Willow! Sal's horse, Willow! I passed my food sack and backpack through the fence and climbed through. Willow pawed the ground and flicked her mane. She recognized me. I approached her slowly, fishing an apple out of my sack and holding it toward her. She backed off a few steps, tossed her head, and whisked her dark tail. She stepped toward me and rubbed the side of her head against my arm.

'You miss Sal, don't you?' I said, stroking her. 'You miss her to pieces, don't you?' Willow was beautiful. I could run up to camp, fetch my wire cutters, return, and take her with me. Then I'd have my horse and I could ride my trail.

Selfish Zinny. Thief!

When I climbed through the other side of the fence, Willow paced back and forth in the enclosure, agitated, restless. She stared after me as I ran up the trail.

On through the remaining portion of Maiden's Walk I went, surprised to exit it alive. Loaded with guilt, full to bursting with it. *If you loved someone and he was sick, how could you help him?* Down through Crow Hollow where the crows were eerily silent. *If you loved someone and he wanted to die, what could you do?*

Across Baby Toe Ridge, staring at the sky so I wouldn't see any dead baby toes. *If you've done something wrong, how do you fix it?*

Over the railroad, past the stumps, on to Sleepy Bear Ridge.

By the time I made my way to my camp, now about fourteen miles up the trail, it was pouring, a real frog-strangler. I crawled under the tarp and lay there listening to the rain smattering against the leaves overhead and dripping onto the tarp. Wind whooshed across the hillside, threatening to rip the tarp from its moorings.

36

Discovered

The low wail of the train whistle awoke me eight hours later. It was still raining and too late to work on the trail. Instead, I decided to move my camp forward, to the grove of larch trees where I'd last worked, near the edge of Spook Hollow, which I'd soon be entering to clear the next section of trail.

The larch grove proved a comforting spot. Overhead, the branches formed a dense canopy, shielding me from the rain, and below was a soft, mossy carpet on a gentle slope. Once everything was set up, I rummaged under leaves and bushes for dry wood and built a small fire, thinking all the while about Uncle Nate, lying there in his bed, trapped.

If Uncle Nate had been meeting some woman up in the hills, maybe the place where the medallion and ring were buried was their secret spot.

No! There was no woman!

I sought a climbing tree, settling on an oak with sturdy branches. Hunched up on a high limb, I had a panoramic view of the hills which fell away below me, down across a wide stretch of grassy knolls and more larch groves, to a farm far, far below.

A *whoop* of the wind reminded me of baby Rose. I could hear her *whoop-whoop-whooping*, gasping for air, or was it me I heard? Was it my own gasping? How silent it had been when it stopped.

A bird landed on a nearby tree and snatched up a caterpillar. And what had the caterpillar snatched up that morning?

Who had *I* caught the whooping cough from? You would think that in all these years, I would have wondered that, but I never had. Someone else had given it to me. I didn't just manufacture it out of the air and hand it to Rose.

Then the scene in the barn, when I'd showed Aunt Jessie the snake, played through my mind. But I had *first* offered her the medallion. Maybe *that* – and not the snake – was what made her wail. Maybe she recognized the medallion. Maybe she knew something about it.

I stared down the hill. Off to my right wound the trail leading back toward home, and to my left hovered the black forest. A movement at the edge of the trees caught my eye, and as I watched, a sleek, spotted bobcat stepped into the clearing. It crept forward, targeting something in the grass ahead. Slowly, purposefully, he moved across the hill, and then he pounced, batting his paws at a dark object. In an instant he grasped his prey in his teeth and pranced back the way he'd come. The animal in his mouth – a mole, it looked like – squirmed, its back legs dancing in the air.

From below came the sound of voices and a deep laugh. Scanning the hillside from my high branch, I spotted two young men coming up the hill. One carried a rifle and a sack. The other was swigging from a bottle and gesturing toward the trees just below me.

The young man with the rifle spotted something, took aim and fired, and there was a sharp crack as the bullet hit a tree. He swore and snatched the bottle from his companion, taking a long drink. The two men moved on up the hill, paused on the trail, and apparently spotted my campsite, for they headed directly for it. By the time I reached them, they were rummaging in my food sack.

'Leave it alone,' I said.

Startled, they turned. Eyeing me, the one with the rifle, and the taller of the two, laughed. 'Who's this?' he said to the one with the bottle. 'A girl scout?'

At close glance they seemed younger, maybe sixteen or seventeen. The shorter boy took a drink and wiped his mouth on the back of his hand, staring me up and down. 'Kinda young to be up here all by herself,' he said.

'I'm not by myself.'

'Oh yeah?' said the shorter one, looking around. 'Don't see no company.'

'My father's here. So are my uncles. They're hunting.' *Jake*, I prayed. *Be near.* But then I remembered the sheriff. Jake might be in jail, for all I knew.

The boy with the rifle listened. 'Don't hear no shots.'

Dad, I prayed, *fly over in that airplane.* But it was Sunday. He'd be at home. 'They're hauling in their catch,' I said.

'Oh yeah, what'd they get?'

'Lots. A bobcat, two deer...' *Aunt Jessie*, I prayed. *Protect me.*

'Ain't deer season. Ain't supposed to be hunting deer,' said the one with the rifle, but he looked impressed.

A warm breeze ruffled my hair. Maybe Aunt Jessie *was* near. I said, 'They're trigger-happy. They'll shoot just about anything. Look – over there – there's one of my uncles.'

They whirled around. 'Where?'

'There – passing through those woods—'

They stared. 'Don't see 'em,' the taller one said.

'What's this?' said the other, waving the bottle in the direction of the already completed portion of the trail. 'A path or something? Where's it go?'

The leaves on the trees fluttered. *Aunt Jessie?* 'Nowhere,' I lied. 'It ends down there a-ways.' Maybe the trail was a bad, bad idea. Now anyone could find their way to our farm. Any sort of vandal or derelict. Any drunken fool with a gun or a knife or—

The short one stepped close to me. I could smell the whisky as he spoke. 'Guess this is your lucky day. Guess we won't be staying around to meet your old man.'

'What's the hurry?' said the other. 'I wanna bag me a bobcat.'

'I saw one,' I said. 'Down there, sneaking off through the trees toward that farm.' It was not the way the bobcat had gone, but I was determined they shouldn't find it.

'Yeah? When?'

'Just before you came.'

'Come on,' he said to the short boy, and he headed in the direction I'd indicated.

The short boy reached forward and ran his hand down my arm. 'Too bad,' he said, with a sickly grin. 'Too bad.' With a low laugh, he took another drink and ambled off after his friend, who was hurrying down the hillside.

Thank you, Aunt Jessie.

I bundled up my belongings, stamped out my fire, and slipped into the woods. It was a dark and forbidding and eerie place, but I wanted to be hidden.

37

Spook Hollow

DO NOT CROSS SPOOK HOLLOW AT NIGHT!
DO NOT TRAVEL ALONE!
WATCH OUT FOR GHOSTS IN TREES!

These were the warnings written on the trail map.

That night at my campsite on the edge of Spook Hollow, every sound and sight mushroomed into ghostly images. Gnarled tree limbs, crooked as a dog's hind leg, became the contorted arms of witches. Vines burst into long, sinuous snakes, and the knobs and knots on tree trunks bulged with the blistered faces of goblins. The wind was the call of ghosts, and the trees were tall, cloaked wizards in high peaked hats.

The next morning's light was only slightly reassuring. Every noise made me flinch, and the faintest movement in the treetops had me ready to fight off ghosts which might drop on my head.

The map showed the trail dipping into Spook Hollow, crossing Bear Alley Creek and continuing up the other side of the hollow, this part of the trail spanning about three miles. Beyond was a mile-long stretch across Shady Death Ridge, and the final two or three miles of the trail swooped down into Donut

Hole, up and over Hogback Hill, across Doolittle Creek and Surrender Bridge into Chocton.

Jumpy as a grasshopper, I could not seem to get started on the trail that day. My head was preoccupied with puzzles.

Where would Uncle Nate meet up with a woman, anyway? At the farm connected to the meadow where I'd cut the fence wires? Maybe they hadn't met in a house at all. *There was no woman!*

They could have met at a special place: in Crow Hollow or on Baby Toe Ridge. Then I remembered the cabin in the larch grove below Sleepy Bear Ridge, and since this was not far from where I'd camped, I decided to investigate it.

It was cool and quiet in the trees behind the cabin: no sounds of anyone moving about. I crept around the side, to a window, but it was boarded up. At the front of the cabin was a small porch. I knocked at the door, knowing that no one was inside. If the door hadn't been locked, I might have gone in.

Then I thought about the two boys I'd run into the day before. This might be their cabin, and if they came back and found me poking around, who knew what they might do? I hurried back to the trail.

OK, Spook Hollow, it's daylight, and I'm coming on through!

For the next three days, I clambered through that hollow, clearing the trail and talking to the ghosts. *Pay no attention to me*, I'd say, *I'll be out of your way in no time at all*. At the slightest noise, I'd resume my speech. *It's just me, Zinny Taylor, trying to make my way along this trail.*

The air was chock-full of birdcalls. The grosbeak's loud *cleeps* and *eeks*, the finch's *chirp-chirp*, and the sparrow's *sweet, sweet, sweet* rolled through the air. The robin's *cheer-up, cheer-up* and the thrush's *ee-oh-lay* punctuated my sweeping. More insistent calls, as if commanding me to stop and take notice, were delivered by chickadees and crows and woodpeckers.

Aunt Jessie and Uncle Nate had taught me to identify all these calls. They would love it up here. They used to come up here together, and I wondered now if Aunt Jessie had really stopped coming because her sugar was acting up. Maybe that's when Uncle Nate had met that woman, replacing Aunt Jessie before she was even gone. *That woman.* I wanted to know who she was and what she looked like and *there was no woman, Zinny, stop it.*

It's just me, ghosts. I've already got enough things haunting me, thank you very much.

At the end of each day, I'd race back to my campsite and follow my usual evening routine, except that I didn't climb any trees here. I didn't want to run into any ghosts lolling around in the branches.

Each day I returned to the cabin, staying a safe distance away. There was no sign of anyone. Where was *that woman*? She lived there, a quiet country lady, just waiting for Uncle Nate to visit.

Maybe she was pining away, not knowing that Uncle Nate was sick and couldn't come. Maybe I should tell her. As soon as I thought this, I felt terrible, as if I were betraying Aunt Jessie. Who did *that woman* think she was, anyway, trying to steal Uncle Nate? She probably wasn't a quiet country lady at all. She was probably young and beautiful with dark-red lipstick and skin-tight clothes.

38

Bear Alley

Maybe I was starting to go loopy up there in the woods all by myself, but more and more I felt as if I were being guarded or protected, and I don't mean by Jake Boone. I'd scouted around each evening and early in the morning, but never saw hide nor hair of him. This was, I hate to say, disappointing. It either meant that Jake was in jail or that he'd started chasing May directly.

I was still seeing those flashes of movement here and there – behind a tree or a bush, or slipping over the edge of a ravine, or around a bend. *Probably a harmless animal*, I'd think. But more and more I thought my Aunt Jessie might be hovering near by. Sometimes I used Uncle Nate's camera to snap pictures of retreating shadows, hoping I'd caught her on film.

At the bottom of Spook Hollow was Bear Alley Creek, tumbling over rocks and winding down toward the Ohio River. On the far side of the creek were more woods, stretching up a steep hillside. I took a break at the creek, sitting beside the river, casting stones and soaking my feet in the cool, clear water. A pair of beavers swam along the far bank, lugging branches to a dam downstream. Water spiders flicked along smooth water below the over-hanging bank.

As I reached for a stone from the damp bank, I noticed a clear print in the earth. It was a footprint, about eight inches long, its toe marks topped with claw prints. I scanned the bank on both sides. On a nearby log was a tuft of black fur caught on the bark.

While I was trying to remember if a bear could climb trees, and while I was checking around for one I might climb if I had to, I saw that the bark on several trees was ripped lengthwise, long claw marks dug into the softer wood beneath. A bear might not be able to climb, but it might try, and it could reach six or seven feet off the ground, from the looks of those claw marks.

And then, on the far side of the stream, there he was, as if dropped from the sky: a big, glossy black bear, his slim head lifted and his brown snout sniffing the air. He looked up and down the bank, and if he saw me, he made no sign of recognition. He stepped forward, his huge feet flopping silently and his wide body lumbering from side to side. He made his way slowly over the rocks and into the stream, where he stood on a flat rock, scanning the water.

With a sudden lurch, he slapped a front paw at the water, dipped his head and came up with a fish, his teeth grasping its middle so that its tail and head flipped on either side of the bear's mouth. The bear carried his catch to the bank, slapped it on the ground and pulled at it with teeth and claws, devouring it in minutes.

I probably should have slipped away to the tree and scrambled high into it, but I was hypnotized by this bear, so oblivious of me sitting there. Again he crept into the stream and snared another fish, which he took to the bank and ate. Then he sat on the bank sniffing the air.

He glanced directly at me – or seemed to – several times, but he also swung his head toward two squirrels chasing each other up a nearby tree, and at a finch pecking at the ground. It was as if we were all just part of the scenery.

The bear snatched one more fish, which he took with him as he lumbered back the way he had come, into the woods on the far side. Although I hadn't had the least fear of him when he was fishing in the stream, I wasn't exactly thrilled that he had gone off in the same direction my trail headed. I wondered if he'd be so mild if I surprised him, if I accidentally came upon him in his territory.

I waited an hour or so to give him time enough to move beyond where I'd be likely to go that day, and then, uneasy, I crossed the stream and worked my way along the new stretch of trail. Frequently I stopped, listened, and scanned the woods around me.

Aunt Jessie, you can protect me if you want. You other ghosts don't need to bother with me.

For the next few days, I carried on. Beyond Spook Hollow was a narrow ridge, Shady Death. I had expected more dark trees, more eerie terrain, but Shady Death was a grassy, clear hillside with only three maple trees to break up its smooth surface.

This note was on the back of the map:

SHADY DEATH
TWO MEN, SEEKING SHADE ON A HOT SUMMER'S
DAY, WERE SLAIN BENEATH THESE TREES.

I hurried on past those trees, and even though it
was hot, and it would have been nice to rest in the
shade, I wasn't inclined to stop under *those* trees.

From Shady Death, the trail dipped into Donut
Hole, an odd little place, where four small hills came
together, forming a round donut-like basin at their
feet. I liked Donut Hole, a quiet, green hideaway,
though I had trouble at the bottom figuring out
which way the trail continued, and had to climb back
up to the top to get my bearings.

On the far side of Donut Hole rose Hogback Hill,
and by the end of the week I had cleared across most
of it – and what a sight awaited me: a long, green
expanse peppered with bright red and yellow and
blue wildflowers stretching down to Doolittle Creek
and, best of all, to Chocton nestled in the valley
below. Chocton!

What I most wanted to do was to barrel my way
through to the finish, but the next day was Saturday,
the day I'd promised to return home to watch Uncle
Nate. I tried to calculate the remaining distance. One
mile? Two? I'd have to come back to finish.

My camp was still on the far side of Spook Hollow,
and on my way back that day, when I was in the
midst of whispering *Don't mind me* pleas to the

spooks of Spook Hollow, I heard a low grumble. Off to one side, near a thicket, was the bear, his snout raised, sniffing the air. He gave a louder grumble, swinging his head in my direction. When he took two steps toward me, I was off like a shot and up the nearest tree so fast you'd have thought I had wings.

He growled, charging the tree, and butting it with his side. It was a hefty oak, but it shook with the bear's weight, and as I scrambled higher, I feared he could knock the tree right over, or shake me out as if I were a monkey.

39

Lost

I was lost in Spook Hollow. The trees moaned in the
dark and bats zipped through the air, swooping out
of nowhere like tiny dark ghosts. I was cold and
hungry, covered in brambles and scratches, scared
out of my wits. My leg and wrist throbbed.

The bear had turned out to be a *she*, not a *he*, and
what I discovered as I clung to a branch near the top
of the tree was that I'd come between a mother and
her cub, who'd been batting a mouse in the leaves
near by. That mother was angry, real angry.

With a sharp sting, I wondered if my mother had
ever been angry at Aunt Jessie, for stepping in
between me and her. I had always thought my mother
didn't mind or didn't care. Maybe I'd been wrong.

The bear batted and rattled my tree for a good
long while as I clung on, praying to anyone I had
ever known, to the ghosts of Spook Hollow, and
even to the trees themselves. *Don't let me die!* I
thought of Aunt Jessie climbing in that drawer and
of Uncle Nate wishing he were dead. *Not me! I'm
not ready!*

When the bear got fed up with bumping my tree,
she stood there grumbling until the cub joined her.

She patted the cub with one clumsy paw and rubbed her face against the cub's face.

Let me finish my trail.

I hated being so helpless up there in the tree, unable to move, to flee, to do anything whatsoever except chatter to ghosts. Maybe I'd be stuck up there for days. Maybe I'd die up there and my body would fall to the ground and the bear would chew it up and the only remains my family would find would be a pile of bones. They'd say, *Is that Zinny, do you think?*

Where was Jake when I needed him? Where was my dad in that dag-blasted airplane – not that he'd see me in these thick woods, but it would be comforting to know he was looking.

And what in the heck was I doing this trail for anyway? What a stupid idea: tossing out zinnia seeds and scrounging along like some demented derelict, scooping up arrowheads and fossils, scavenging for medallions and lost rings. Why couldn't I give up the trail and go home?

Let me finish. Let me finish something good. Let me find . . . What? Who?

Finally, finally, the bear ambled off, nudging the cub in front of her. By now it was dark, and I waited, wondering if she'd return, if maybe she was faking me out. I wasn't going to be stupid enough to climb down yet. Oh, I was tired. I wanted to close my eyes and sleep a long sleep.

I shifted in the tree and slipped – *whish* – through branches – *thunk* – hitting a branch – *whish* – through more branches – *thunk*. Whish – thunk –

whish. I landed hard and jumped up, looking for the bear.

Nothing out there – and *everything* out there: dark shapes, crooked shapes, menacing shapes. I slipped off through the trees, away from the trail and from the direction the bear had gone, hoping to cut below the trail and back to it. But after an hour or two, I was so turned around that I had no idea where I was – for all I knew I was going in circles and would end up at the bear's den.

That sound – had someone called by name?

In this tired and demented state, I saw her: *Aunt Jessie*. She was standing – or floating, rather – near some trees, and as I went toward her, she moved on, leading me through the woods, but never letting me catch her. In a small clearing, she spread out her arms, or so it seemed, and vanished. I lay down in the clearing and slept.

At daybreak, I made out the shape of the Sleepy Bear Rock high above on the ridge. I was well below the trail, in one of the larch groves, surprised to be alive, surprised to feel so comforted: I had seen Aunt Jessie!

40

Get That Horse

When I saw the cabin, I was so tired and hungry I
didn't care who lived there. I kicked at the door but
couldn't budge it.

'Anybody around?' I called. 'Hey . . .'

I pulled at the shuttered windows, but they were
too firmly fastened. All I could see through a slim
crack was a shelf on the opposite wall. On it: a pot,
a book, and – there beside the shelf – oh there –
on a hook – oh, it was wonderful, oh, it was terrible,
terrible. It was Aunt Jessie's coat.

I was out of there so fast I could have caught air.

I stopped at my campsite only long enough to grab
the wire cutters, a length of rope, and some apples
before starting for home. On the way, I was going
to get that horse.

*Oh that coat! The sight of that coat! That instant
joy, that instant horror!*

I ran down the trail, past Sleepy Bear Rock again,
across Baby Toe Ridge, through Crow Hollow, on
and on. I thought *Aunt Jessie's alive! She lives there!*
I tore down the trail. *No. Someone else has her coat.
Uncle Nate gave her coat to that woman!*

When I reached the meadow, there was Willow,
pawing and pacing. I coaxed her to take an apple,

and she didn't much like my putting a rope on her, but when I cut the fence and led her through, she swung her head high and proud, as if to say, *Out of there at last!* We rode down the trail toward home, where I tied her to a tree by the creek before going on to the house.

'Zinny! We've been waiting!' Bonnie said. 'We're going to the circus, and we thought you forgot. You have to watch Uncle Nate. And guess what – Jake was arrested! Isn't it awful? He's not in jail now, but he might have to go to Juvenile Court. Isn't it awful? Do you think he'll go to jail?'

Sam said, 'Jake stole a *car*. He's in big trouble.'

'Tell her about Bingo,' Ben said.

'Oh!' Bonnie said. 'Ben saw Bingo – you'll never guess where! In Mr Butler's car! Ben thinks Mr Butler stole our Bingo, but Dad doesn't think that could possibly be.'

'We're going to find out, though,' Ben said.

'Right!' Bonnie said. 'Dad says we can go over to the Butlers' after the circus.'

My old spaghetti swamp was so tangled it was as if someone had thrown me in it and tied me up in a zillion knots.

'There you are, Zinny,' Mom said. 'You look a wreck! Are you OK?'

'Sure,' I lied.

'Did the kids tell you about Jake? Honestly, I don't know what to think.'

'Mom,' Gretchen complained, 'May's wearing my jeans. Make her take them off.'

'Zinny, let me sort out Uncle Nate's stuff with you. He has to take this medicine three times—'

Will pulled on my sleeve. 'Jake was arrested.'

May hovered near the door. 'He didn't actually steal that car. He just borrowed it. I know the whole story. He confided in me.' She said this with a studied air, as if it were extremely significant.

'Zinny,' Dad said, 'we have to talk when we get home—'

'Aren't we going to the circus?' Sam wailed.

After they'd left, I slipped into Uncle Nate's room. 'Lucky you,' I said. 'I'm in charge of you today.'

'I know it.'

The phone rang. 'I'll be right back,' I said.

'Ain't going nowhere,' he mumbled.

'That's what you think.'

It was Jake's mother, who wanted to know if Jake was at our house. When I said he wasn't, she said, 'Are you sure – which one are you?'

'Zinny. Yes, I'm sure. No one here but me and Uncle Nate.'

'That boy will be the death of me yet. He's supposed to be grounded, and I mean grounded, except to go to work. He didn't come home last night, and Mrs Flint just called and said he hasn't shown up for work. I'm calling the sheriff. Are you sure he isn't there?'

'I'm sure. Just me and Uncle Nate. You don't think anything has happened to Jake, do you?' I asked.

'I don't know what to think. If you see him, tell

him to get over to that store right away. And Zinny . . .'

'Yes?'

'Tell him he's got a lick of explaining to do.'

From my closet, I snatched the medallion that I'd taken from the metal box in Uncle Nate's drawer, and then I went up to the barn where I knew there was an old bridle. I had hoped there might be a saddle, too, but there wasn't. I retrieved Willow, led her down to the house, and tied her to the porch railing.

'OK, Uncle Nate, let's get a move on. We're going for a ride.'

'Do I look like I'm in any condition for a dag-blasted ride?'

'You said you wanted to go on the trail . . .'

His eyes opened wide.

'I saw her,' I said. 'I saw Aunt Jessie.' I guess I should have told him what else I saw, but I didn't.

'Tarnation!' He swung his legs over the side of the bed and tried to stand. 'Dag-blasted legs.'

I had second thoughts. 'How are you ever going to make it? You can't do it—'

'I can!' he said. 'You gotta take me.'

'But your leg—'

'You gotta, pumpkin. You gotta!'

I pulled him upright and, inch by inch, we made it to the porch, though Uncle Nate had to stop every few feet and lean against the wall. 'My heart's a-jumping,' he said. 'Where'd that horse come from?

You're not going to try to get me on that thing, are you?'

It wasn't easy, but Willow was obliging and patient as I pushed and pulled and shoved Uncle Nate up on her back and climbed up behind him.

'Ain't it supposed to have a saddle?' he said.

'We've got these reins – don't need a saddle.'

'Let's go then,' he said. 'Let's get a move on . . .'

41

The Ride

At the edge of the creek, when I turned the horse up the start of the trail, Uncle Nate said, 'You taking me up there? Way up there?'

'That's where I saw Aunt Jessie, so that's where we're going.'

'OK,' he said, 'but you're awful bossy lately.'

On up the trail we rode under an overcast sky.

He kept slumping forward against the mare's neck and I had to pull him upright, fearing that he'd slide off. He insisted on clutching his stick, which regularly poked my leg.

'Can't we drop that stick?' I asked him.

'Nope. Might need it.' It jabbed my foot. 'Lookee there, you've gone and cleared the whole dag-blasted trail. Why'd you go and do that? Where does this lead anyway?'

'You know this trail perfectly well,' I said.

'Don't talk about it.'

'You've been up here lots and lots of times.'

'Not this way,' he said. 'Not on this-here trail.'

At the spot where I'd discovered the medallion, I pulled over. 'See that rock? You'll never guess what I found there—'

'I know what you found.'

'You do?' I said. 'What?'

He waved his stick at the hole. 'That thingy – that coin thingy.'

'Where'd it come from?' I asked. 'Who put it there? Do you know?'

Uncle Nate craned his neck around to look at me. 'Pumpkin, *you* put it there. Are you being a noodle?'

That chill, that shiver returned. 'When?' I asked. 'When did I put it there? And why? And—'

'Hold your taters,' he said. 'I cain't keep track of all those questions. You don't remember putting it there? You don't remember how you scared us all half to death?'

I saw myself running, running. I was very small. Something was in my hand. I could feel it there pressed against my palm. Rose had been in the drawer—

'Pumpkin?' Uncle Nate said. 'You remember?'

I had touched Rose's hand and when I did, I saw the leather pouch beneath it, and inside the pouch, the medallion. That hand, it was so stiff, so unlike Rose's hand. I grabbed the pouch and left the house. Out of the house, up the hill.

'Pumpkin?' Uncle Nate repeated. 'It was when Rose died—'

'Shh,' I said. 'Wait . . .' I wanted to see how much more I could remember. Running, running, tripping, falling, stumbling. Clawing at the dirt, burying the pouch, finding the stone to mark the spot, sitting there calling, 'Rose, Rose, Rose . . .'

Uncle Nate said, 'We couldn't find you – it was terrible, terrible . . .'

I couldn't remember anything more. 'Who found me?'

'Me and Jessie. We found you sitting there. We took you home—'

'So how did you know what I'd buried there?'

'I'm nosy,' Uncle Nate said. 'I came back. I looked.'

We rode on through the hills, into Maiden's Walk. I was thinking about the medallion, fingering it in my pocket, wondering why it had been in Rose's hand, and why I kept seeing two medallions in my mind. Around the edges of these thoughts, I saw glimpses of a circus tent, like the one my family might be entering now.

We reached the meadow and approached it cautiously, to be sure the owner hadn't yet discovered his missing mare or his clipped fence. No sign of anyone.

Uncle Nate said, 'Somebody oughta mend that fence,' and then, 'What're you doing? Ride *around* it.'

'We're riding the trail, and the trail goes through here.'

'Did you put these stones in here? Where'd you get this horse?'

'Uncle Nate – was there another medallion – were there two of them?'

'Pumpkin, I cain't talk about it . . .' He stared straight ahead.

'But why not? Do you know what the initials meant – TNWM?'

'Till Next We Meet...' There was a catch in his voice, a muffled low sound at the back of his throat.

Till Next We Meet, Till Next We Meet. I saw the circus again, a tent, a table with a brightly coloured cloth. I saw two medallions.

In the distance, dark clouds were gathering, and I nudged the horse into a slow trot. 'Bumpy dang thing,' Uncle Nate said, sliding this way and that. 'My heart's jumping.' On we went, through the rest of Maiden's Walk, and through Crow Hollow.

'Uncle Nate, where did you go, you and Aunt Jessie, when you came up here...?'

He shook his head. 'Cain't...'

'And why did Aunt Jessie stop coming?'

'Her legs was bothering her.'

We crossed Baby Toe Ridge, where we stopped and gave the horse a rest. The wind whipped across the hillside, and I wished I'd thought to bring jackets. Uncle Nate was shivering.

'Shouldn't be out riding in my pyjamas,' he said.

'We'd better turn back,' I said. 'This isn't a good idea—'

He waved his stick in the air. 'We ain't turning back! We ain't! We're going up there...'

'Have you been meeting someone up here?' I asked.

He tapped my leg with his stick. 'You're so dang nosy all of a sudden—'

'Were you?' I pressed. 'Were you?'

He whispered, 'Yes.'

He might as well have hit me over the head with a sack of coal. 'What's she like?'

'What're you talking about?'

'The woman – *that woman* – the one you were meeting.'

'You are out of your noodle, pumpkin!'

'Zinn-eee! Zinn-eee!'

Shouts came from beyond the railroad tracks, nearly sending us out of our skins. I think we both thought it was a ghost. Willow's ears flattened against her head.

'Zinn-eee! Zinn-eee!'

'Should I answer?' I said.

Uncle Nate gripped his stick. 'Well, we cain't just dig ourselves a hole . . .'

I called out, 'Helloooo . . .'

Straggling toward us came Jake, covered in briars and scratches. 'Zinny, Zinny!'

'What happened? What's the matter?' I thought maybe he'd murdered someone, from the look of him.

'Zinny! Where've you *been*? I've been up here all night looking for you. I thought maybe you got lost or got eaten by a bear or – or who knows what could have happened to you. You weren't supposed to go home again yet. It hasn't been ten days.'

Had it been Jake's voice I heard calling me last night? 'Mom *asked* me to come home today. I'm watching Uncle Nate. And what are you doing up here?'

'Aww, Zinny . . .' He put his hand on my arm. 'I couldn't help it. I didn't want you to be all by yourself.'

I remembered May standing in the kitchen saying, *I know the whole story. He confided in me.* I slugged Jake. 'Let go,' I said. 'I've gotta take Uncle Nate somewhere.'

'Then I'm coming too.'

'It's a dag-blasted party,' Uncle Nate said. 'Hey, Zinny, where'd you get this horse?'

42

The Cabin

Uncle Nate was quiet as we turned off the trail and rode down through the larch groves, with Jake walking beside us. 'I saw Aunt Jessie down there,' I said, 'at the bottom of the hill.'

'She sure gets around,' Jake said.

I pulled up in sight of the cabin. I wasn't sure what to think, any more. I didn't know what to expect.

Uncle Nate stared at the cabin. 'I made it!' he said. 'I made it!' He twisted and fidgeted, trying to get off the horse.

'Wait a sec—' I said. 'Wait . . .'

'What's this all about?' Jake asked.

I wanted to turn around and go home.

'My heart's a-jumping,' Uncle Nate said.

'Zinny, does he look funny? Nate?'

Uncle Nate lay on the bed in the cabin, as Jake and I tried to revive him. Jake had kicked in the door and carried Uncle Nate inside. I feared Uncle Nate was going to die. Had I done it again?

'Jake – he's going to live, right?' I said. 'He'll be OK, right?'

Jake didn't answer. He searched for Uncle Nate's pulse. 'Nate? Nate?'

Everything was swirling around: the bed and Uncle Nate and Jake. Pictures on a dresser, cushions on a chair, toys, the coat.

I grabbed Uncle Nate's hand. 'You'd better not die. You'd better talk to me.'

He mumbled something which I couldn't understand.

'Hear that?' I said. 'He's trying to talk. He's not going to die, is he?'

Uncle Nate whispered, 'Our place.'

'Whose place? Who lives here?'

He blinked. 'Rose . . . and Jessie . . . and me . . .'

I shrank back, staring at him.

'Cripes!' Jake said. 'Cripes!'

Uncle Nate blinked. 'No drawer . . .' He tapped my wrist. He seemed very earnest; he wanted me to understand.

'Uncle Nate? The drawer . . .? Why did Aunt Jessie climb in the drawer? Did I scare her? Was it the snake?'

He didn't answer.

'Was it the medallion – was that it? Because she had last seen it in Rose's hand . . .?

'In the barn,' he whispered, 'she thought you were Rose . . .'

'But I wasn't! I'm not! I'm not Rose!'

'Rose coming to get her . . .'

I could hardly bear it. 'How awful, how terrible . . .'

He tapped my wrist again. 'No – she *wanted* Rose – she *wanted* to see her . . .'

'Cripes!' Jake said.

'Three nights,' Uncle Nate said, 'three nights she heard Rose calling. Rose said, "Get ready . . ." '

'Cripes!' Jake said.

Uncle Nate said, 'That doctor said Jessie had a diabetic comma . . .'

'Coma, you mean?'

'Whatever . . . She forgot to take her insulin – or she took her insulin and forgot to eat, one of those, and that doctor said she went into that diabetic comma thing.' His eyelids fluttered. 'But I know better. She was pining for Rose . . .' Uncle Nate closed his eyes.

It hadn't been my fault. He didn't blame me. This hit me like a huge wave breaking down on me, washing me over, pushing me to shore. But still, I didn't like to think that I had been there, living and breathing, and still she might have preferred to be with Rose. 'What about *me*?' I said.

'Pumpkin, you've *got* a mother . . .' He groaned once, and drifted off.

Prickly stings went all through me. I turned away. 'Do something!' I begged Jake. He leaned over Uncle Nate. As he did so, the row of pictures on the dresser caught my eye. I looked closer. I knew these people.

There was Aunt Jessie and Uncle Nate. There was baby Rose. Dozens of framed photographs. Aunt Jessie's lotions. Her perfume. Her hand mirror.

I felt so cold, so cold.

Aunt Jessie's coat on the hook. Her sewing basket on the floor. And there, beside the wardrobe was a shopping bag, and in it were toys and stuffed animals. I lifted them out, one by one. They were familiar to me. I'd seen them, handled them, played with them.

On the shelf, in the pot, was a tiny baby bracelet with the letters R-O-S-E, resting on a pink crocheted bonnet. The book next to it was an album filled with photographs of baby Rose: cradled in Aunt Jessie's arms; lying on a white blanket; sitting next to Uncle Nate on the sofa – on and on. And then, there it was: a photograph of me and baby Rose, hobbling across the living room doing the old lady.

Next to the pot and the album was the little black box, and in it was Jake's ring. I snatched it up, handed it to Jake.

'Cripes . . .'

'Zinny – pumpkin,' Uncle Nate whispered.

Jake clutched Uncle Nate's hand. I leaned close.

'That ring was from Rose.' He gurgled. 'Rose was calling . . .' His mouth formed a thin smile. 'I like it here, and I'll like it over yonder, but . . .' Again his arms twitched. 'I don't wanna be in that drawer . . .'

I glanced back at the dresser, but as I did so, Uncle Nate's whole body jerked and convulsed, and then he was still and quiet and I feared he was gone, gone, gone.

43

Drawers

Jake took the horse and raced to find my parents, while I stayed with Uncle Nate. His eyes were closed, his body still, and on his face the look of purest calm, as if he'd finally gotten to the place he'd been longing for. He wasn't dead, but I was afraid that death would slip in the way night overtakes day, subtly, quietly. I opened the drawers of the dresser one by one. In the thin top drawer were dozens of letters. They all began: *To my dearest Rose*. Some ended, *From your loving mother*, and the rest ended with *From your loving Pa*.

They were written over the course of the last nine years, ever since Rose had died. They were alternately newsy:

WE PLANTED CORN TODAY,

and affectionate:

YOUR SKIN IS LIKE SILK,

and filled with longing:

WE MISS YOU SO . . .

Many of them mentioned me:

ZINNY CAN READ! SHE READ THE WHOLE OF YOUR

Baby Bear book to us tonight. Are you reading, Rose?

and:

Today Zinny found two brachiopods, but she calls them 'broken pods'. We saved one for you.

and:

Zinny has the flu, and we are terribly, terribly worried. Are you well, Rose?

In the second and third drawers were baby Rose's clothes, from infant gowns to the dresses and rompers of a four-year-old. All were neatly folded, and scattered among them were sprigs of lavender.

I wasn't prepared for what was in the bottom drawer. When I pulled it open, I cringed. There, lying side by side, were me and baby Rose. Our hands were pressed together in a friendly clasp.

These were the dolls Aunt Jessie had made, but they were so lifelike, so rounded and soft like real toddlers, that it wasn't hard to imagine that they were real children sleeping.

I touched their clasped hands, and as I did so, a coin slipped from within. It was a duplicate of the medallion, with *TNWM* engraved on it.

Till Next We Meet. And then more of the memory poured forth, in a stream of images. We'd been at the circus, Rose and I and Aunt Jessie and Uncle

Nate. We'd stopped in a fortune-teller's booth and gazed into her crystal ball. She'd held our hands, examined our palms, Rose's and mine. The fortune-teller had pressed a medallion into each of our palms, and she'd said, '*Till Next We Meet.*'

I had touched Rose's hand in the drawer and taken her medallion. I'd run through the woods and I'd buried it. And later – days? weeks? – I'd taken my own medallion and pressed it into Aunt Jessie's hand. 'For Rose,' I'd said, and Aunt Jessie had hugged me, hugged me so hard and so long, and I didn't want her to stop.

And remembering this, I could feel Aunt Jessie there in the cabin, near Uncle Nate lying so still on the bed, and I could feel Rose there, too. I took Rose's medallion from my pocket, and my own medallion from the cabin drawer, and I held them a long time, a long, long, long time.

It seemed a shame that Aunt Jessie and Uncle Nate spent so much time chasing the dead. And yet, I could see how they were trying so hard to keep the dead alive, to defy that darkness sweeping in and overtaking them.

I went over to Uncle Nate and put my face up close to his. 'Uncle Nate? Uncle Nate – *Make the company jump! Make that dag-blasted company jump!*'

One eye opened. Closed. Opened. He said, 'You gonna put that pillow over my face again?'

44

Petunia

When my parents arrived, Uncle Nate was sitting up in bed, looking through the photo album with me.

'Just had a little spell, is all . . .' he told them.

Dad said, 'Maybe you ought to spend the night in the hospital.'

'That's about as likely as a hog taking wing,' Uncle Nate said.

'How are you going to get back down that trail, anyway?' Mom asked.

'Same way I got up here, on that horse.'

'Where *is* the horse?' I said. 'Where's Jake? How'd you find us?'

'Mm . . .' Dad said. 'Jake showed us where to go. Then he went along with the sheriff.'

'The sheriff? Why the sheriff?'

Dad cleared his throat. 'Seems there was something about a stolen horse . . .?'

Oh, Jake!

Dad, Mom, and I spent the night in the cabin with Uncle Nate.

In the morning, at first light, we carried Uncle Nate down through the larch grove to where Dad had left his car, at the side of a dirt road at the bottom of a long hill. When we got home, there was the sheriff, waiting to talk to me about 'matters concerning trespassing and a stolen horse'.

Jake, he said, was in real trouble. First, the car, and now trespassing and stealing the horse. When I told the sheriff that I was responsible for the fence and that I'd taken the horse, my parents nearly fainted away there in our kitchen.

If we lived in a bigger town, Jake and I probably would have had to go to Juvenile Court to tell our different stories. Instead, because this was Bybanks, we spent the afternoon with the sheriff, trying to explain. It was such a muddle, what with Jake going on about how he had only wanted to give me presents to get my attention, and me trying to explain about the trail and the hand of God and Aunt Jessie, baby Rose, and Uncle Nate.

The sheriff said he had a powerful headache. He ordered us to go home and write down our separate accounts of what we had done and why we had done it. After he had a chance to read these, he'd decide on our punishment. Meanwhile, we had to repair the fence (Willow had already been returned to her owner), and the sheriff said I'd better finish the trail.

A week later, I did finish it. I cleared on down Hogback Hill, and across Surrender Bridge on Doolittle Creek. The exact end of the trail was just a little bit further on, the final stone unearthed in the back garden of the mayor of Chocton, who was not particularly pleased to see me clearing away his prized lavender border. When I told him this was one end of the historic Bybanks–Chocton Trail, however, his ears perked up. He made his wife come out and take a picture of him standing beside the final stone, and then, as an afterthought, he allowed her to take a picture of him and me together, beside the trail.

He immediately phoned *The Chocton Herald*, who sent over a reporter and a photographer. The following week, an article appeared. Suddenly our phone was ringing off the wall, with people wanting to talk to Petunia. The reporter had my name wrong. Instead of Zinnia, it was Petunia. Typical.

Another reporter called, astounded that I'd cleared the trail all on my own. 'Why did you do it?' he asked.

I didn't think he'd understand about the hand of God any more than the sheriff would have, and I didn't want to tell him about Aunt Jessie and Uncle Nate and baby Rose and the medallions. The only thing I could think of to say was, 'I like it up there. You can hear yourself think.'

The following week, I put up a wooden sign at each end of the trail, identifying it as *The Redbird Trail*.

Strangers started using the trail. One day two women clomped onto our porch asking to use the bathroom. 'There's no facilities on that trail,' they said.

The next day, two boys asked for Band-Aids for the blisters on their feet, and an elderly man asked for a ride home. 'Didn't realize it was so far,' he said. 'Thought there'd at least be a bus at this end to take people back to Chocton. Why isn't there a bus?'

One day the Butler family showed up: Bill Butler, Mrs Butler, and Old Mrs Butler. With them was Gobbler. 'It's really Bingo,' Ben said. 'Did you know that, Zinny? Jake told us all about it.'

Bill Butler asked if he could leave Gobbler and Old Mrs Butler on our porch while he and his wife went up the trail. My parents were beginning to lose it. 'Something's got to be done about this,' my father said. 'We've got strangers in our bathroom, old ladies on our porch – why, today somebody asked if he could borrow my jacket because he'd forgotten his!'

Jake and I were each assigned a hundred hours of community service to atone for our stealing. Each week, Jake had to wash Mrs Foster's 'beaut' of a car, groom and walk Bingo, and work one free hour for Mrs Flint. My job was to keep the Redbird Trail clear of trash from all the new hikers who were using it.

I tried to tell the sheriff that I would have done that anyway, without being told to, and maybe he should assign me something else in addition, but he told me not to argue with him. Then he said, 'I thought you were the one who didn't talk much.'

Alone, I hiked the whole length of the trail, scooping up trash and propping up trampled zinnias. When I got to Surrender Bridge, I stood there studying that water running underneath. It was an odd feeling, knowing I was done, knowing I'd cleared the whole trail.

I looked back up the hill, and in my mind I saw

that trail winding through the hills, up and down, in and out, all the way back to Bybanks. Every spot on that trail was part of me.

For several glorious minutes there, I was about the happiest person on the face of this planet. The trail was beautiful and it was good. I looked up into the trees and the sky, and the sky was vast and wide. I heard, in my head, the soft refrain of a song Aunt Jessie used to sing:

> LAY YOUR BURDEN DOWN, GIRL,
> LAY YOUR BURDEN DOWN.
> IN THE SOFT COOL MORNING,
> LAY YOUR BURDEN DOWN.

And then I had the oddest feeling, warm and comforting, as if a gentle hand had reached down from the heavens and stroked my hair.

45

Chicory

Uncle Nate was getting better each day. He was walking around with a cane in one hand and his stick in the other. Since he might not be able to make it up the trail for a while, he said I could bring the photo albums down from the cabin. He wanted to have those pictures beside him. They were his medicine, he said.

I wondered if he'd start chasing his Redbird again when his leg mended. In a way, I hoped he wouldn't. I hoped he'd just stay close to us. But it was hard to imagine him giving up his chase; it was hard to believe he wouldn't catch her one day.

One evening in September, we were all sitting around the table eating spaghetti, and I was talking about seeing Aunt Jessie in the larch grove, but only Ben and Uncle Nate believed me. I had hoped my pictures would offer proof that I'd seen her up in the woods, but when I had them developed, there was no sign of her in any of them. A couple pictures showed a flash of red, which I tried to tell my family was her hair, but they insisted it was a bird or a leaf.

Ben and Uncle Nate, however, studied the pictures closely.

'I think that's her all right,' Ben said, tapping a dot of red.

'Of course it's her!' Uncle Nate said. 'Any noodle can see that!'

Will said, 'Zinny, you're getting just like Uncle Nate, you know that? Proof! Hah! Like that picture Uncle Nate took . . .'

Uncle Nate tapped Will on the shoulder. 'Well, if Jessie didn't take that picture of me, who did?'

No one had an answer for that.

And it seemed there were a whole lot worse things than to become like Uncle Nate. I kind of liked the idea of me dashing around with a stick and a camera, chasing someone I love.

I swirled my spaghetti around my fork, eyeing those meatballs buried underneath. That spaghetti swirled around in loops and waves. You could follow one strand to its end and then you could hop to the next piece and the next and the next. I stabbed a meatball, and bit into it, anticipating that delicious bonus, but instead I chomped down on a piece of gristle. 'Eck . . .'

'Zinny,' Ben said, bending close to me. 'You have your good meatballs, and then you have your bad meatballs . . .'

Exactly.

Ben was beside himself one day when he discovered plants growing in his squirt garden, right where he'd planted the eggs. A couple weeks later, when pale-blue flowers emerged, Ben raced to the library for a wildflower book and came home waving it and shouting. 'Look! It's chicory! It grew from chicken eggs!'

There on the open page was a chicory plant, identical to the ones growing in Ben's garden. The description beneath included the legend of Chicory, who was once a lady named Florilor. Florilor was turned into a flower because she rejected the sun god's love. As a flower, Florilor/Chicory opens up until noon, watching for the sun god, but when he is overhead, she closes her petals, ignoring him.

Another legend claimed that the seeds could be used as a love potion. If you fed them to someone, you could get them to love you.

Dad confessed to me that he planted the chicory. He thought it was funny, but he didn't dare admit that he planted it, because Ben took it all very seriously. Ben was doing a report on it for school. I wasn't sure what his teacher would make of his claim that chicory grows from chicken eggs.

One day I got a good 'meatball' in the mail. It was a postcard from my friend Sal Hiddle, with this one line: *Coming home to Bybanks!*

In a burst of unaccountable goodwill that same day, I gave away all my collections: the bottle caps and buttons went to Sam; the lucky stones to Will; the bookmarks to Gretchen; the coloured pencils to May; the shoelaces and bottles to Ben; and the keys and postcards to Bonnie. No one, not even Gretchen or May, said anything about their new collections being *immature*. I was surprised by that.

The woman at the historical museum was beside

herself with excitement over the flints, arrowheads, and fossils from the trail. Her nose had been deep in books ever since, researching my finds. Occasionally I went in to help her, but it was hard to stay in that musty room very long.

I planned on putting Poke and his mate in my closet, in a box, to hunker down for the winter, and hoped the cricket would find its way into the house and spend the winter with us too. Jake said it was good luck, to have a cricket on your hearth. At first I thought he said 'a cricket on your heart', which seemed a bit odd, but when he repeated it, I heard him right.

One day, not long after I'd finished the trail, Jake came over and sat with me on the porch swing. I'd been dreaming about Jake, wishing for him to come.

We swung back and forth in silence for a while. At last he put his hands together and said, 'Zinny, I want to tell you something.'

My heart was thumping away.

'You said I was a dag-blasted fool—' he began.

'I didn't really mean—'

'And maybe you were right,' he said. 'Maybe I just lost my head.'

'That can happen,' I said, wishing he'd stop talking. I prepared my mouth to receive a kiss.

'Maybe you were right about something else, too.'

'Mm . . .?' I got my lips ready.

'Maybe I'm too old for you,' he said, staring out across the yard.

'Not *that* old – just a few years—'

'Don't try to make me feel less foolish.'

'But . . .'

He chewed on his lip. 'I'm sorry if I embarrassed you.'

May leaned out the upstairs window. 'Jake?'

He stood up and leaned back to get a better view. 'Hi,' he said.

'You wanted to see me?' she asked.

'Yup.'

'I'll be right down!' she yelped.

'*What?*' I said. 'What do you want to see May for?'

He rubbed his hands through his hair and scratched the back of his neck and chewed on his lip some more. 'I thought I'd ask May to the movies. That ought to make *you* happy.' He grinned, then instantly frowned. 'Get me out of *your* hair, at least!'

I grabbed his arm. 'Jake Boone,' I said. 'If you take May to the movies, I'll punch your brains in.'

Oh, the look on his face! You'd have thought I'd slung a bucket of hog slop on him.

'I mean it, Jake Boone,' I said. 'If you go and tangle up my spaghetti again, I'll shove ten tons of chicory down your throat!'

'Spaghetti?' he said. 'Chicory?' He stared at me. 'Are you trying to tell me you *like* me?'

May burst through the door. 'Here I am!' she announced.

'Cripes!' Jake said.

46

The Chase

Up on the trail is the most beautiful sight you ever did see. The zinnias are like bright little sentries marching along the trail, and the trees have burst forth in brilliant reds and yellows, so that all around you is an explosion of colour. I know the leaves will fall soon, and our squirt gardens will fade, and I wish I could freeze it, capture it. I hope I can save it all in my mind, until the spring, when things will bloom all over again.

And even when I'm not on the trail, it's with me, in my mind. On the trail I can think, and on the trail I am me, and on the trail I can touch the ground and climb to the sky.

Sometimes I wonder about other trails. Maybe I'll check at the museum for more maps. I can see myself running across the whole country, chasing – what? Who?

Uncle Nate has left the cabin in my care, for the time being, until he can get back up there. He said I could take the family there to show them the shrine to baby Rose and Aunt Jessie. My brothers and sisters were pretty surprised to see all that stuff up there. Mom and Dad, even though they'd seen it before, cried. And after they'd all left, I stayed behind, and I curled up on the bed, hugging the dolls, as if I were four years old.

But now, Jake and I go up there from time to time. One day we had this conversation on the way up the trail:

Jake said, 'I guess you don't know me all that well . . .'

That boy could steal your heart. I said, 'Jake Boone! If I were blindfolded and you came in the room, I'd know it was you – I know what you sound like, smell like. I'd just know it was Jake Boone filling up that room!'

His face turned about thirty-three shades of red, but he said, 'And if I was blindfolded, and you walked in the room – cripes, I'd know it was you from three miles away! If I was blindfolded in Chocton, and you walked into a room in Bybanks, why, I'd know it—'

'OK, Jake, I get the picture . . .'

We were getting a little sappy, but sometimes a little sap is nice. I wouldn't want to *drown* in it, though.

Since then, we've had picnics on the porch and in the larch groves, and one day we cleaned the cabin from top to bottom, but we put all baby Rose's stuff back where we'd found it. Except for the dolls. Baby Rose and baby Zinny, each holding her own medallion, sit side by side on the bed. I figured they'd appreciate a little air.

It feels good to run up that trail with Jake, and it feels good to go in the cabin and remember baby Rose and Aunt Jessie. All kinds of memories are coming back, whole drawers full of them. It doesn't seem weird or morbid to be up there; it seems somehow necessary, at least for a time.

Sometimes I think I see Aunt Jessie and baby Rose running through the hills together, and sometimes I race down the hill after them. I know they aren't *really* there, that this is an image in my mind, one that I *want* to see. I am not completely loopy. But I do often think that there's a very fine line between people in your head and 'real' people out there.

Meanwhile, I think I'm going to teach Jake how to do the boogie-woogie. *Tootle-ee-ah-dah*, I'll tell him, and maybe he'll answer me. Maybe he'll say, *Make that company jump!*

Sharon Creech
Walk Two Moons

Just over a year ago, my father plucked me up like a weed and took me and all our belongings (no, that is not true – he did not bring the chestnut tree or the willow or the maple or the hayloft or the swimming hole or any of those things which belong to me) and we drove three hundred miles straight north and stopped in front of a house in Euclid, Ohio.

There, Salamanca Hiddle begins to unravel the mystery that surrounds her world – a world from which her mother has suddenly, and without warning, disappeared.

'A powerful, emotional narrative which keeps the reader guessing right up to the end.'
Smarties Prize judges

'A really satisfying book – funny, poignant, cunning in the unravelling of its mysteries.'
Observer

Winner of the Newbery Medal
Winner of Children's Book of the Year (Longer Novels)
Shortlisted for the Smarties Book Prize
Winner of WH Smith Mind Boggling Books Award

Sharon Creech
Absolutely Normal Chaos

So. Here it is. My summer journal. As you can see, I got a little carried away.

The problem is this, though. I don't want you to read it.

I really mean it. I just wanted you to know I did it. I didn't want you to think I was one of those kids who says, 'Oh yeah, I did it, but I lost it/my dog ate it/my little brother dropped it in the toilet.'

But please, PLEEEASE DON'T READ IT! How was I to know all this stuff was going to happen this summer? Sigh.

PLEASE DON'T READ IT. I mean it.

Sincerely,

Mary Lou Finney

Would you want *your* teacher to read your summer diary?

'A stonkingly good read!' *Just Seventeen*

A selected list of titles available from Macmillan and Pan Books

The prices shown below are correct at the time of going to press. However, Macmillan Publishers reserve the right to show new retail prices on covers which may differ from those previously advertised.

All Macmillan titles can be ordered at your local bookshop or are available by post from:

**Book Service by Post
PO Box 29, Douglas, Isle of Man IM99 1BQ**

Credit cards accepted. For details:
Telephone: 01624 675137
Fax: 01624 670923
E-mail: bookshop@enterprise.net

Free postage and packing in the UK.
Overseas customers: add £1 per book (paperback)
and £3 per book (hardback).